BEST
WOMEN'S
EROTICA
2010

BEST
WOMEN'S
EROTICA
2010

Edited by

VIOLET BLUE

CLEIS
PRESS

Published in the United States.
Cleis Press Inc., P.O. Box 14697, San Francisco, California 94114.

Printed in the United States.
Cover design: Scott Idleman
Cover photograph: Samantha Wolov
Text design: Frank Wiedemann
Cleis logo art: Juana Alicia
First Edition.
10 9 8 7 6 5 4 3 2 1

ISBN 13: 978-1-57344-373-9

CONTENTS

INTRODUCTION:
THE CHOCOLATE TASTER

More than once in the eight years that I've been an erotica editor, someone has compared my job to that of a chocolate taster. It's a dream job, especially if you have a sweet tooth, and a full-on fantasy every day if you love chocolate. You can study the art of chocolatiering, and nerd out on how chocolate is made, the history of cocoa (violent, romantic and exciting), and go so far as to become ecologically minded and educate people on the greening of chocolate (fair trade cocoa, eco-friendly processes).

It sounds like a world full of sweet, endless possibilities; a job that would never resemble the drudgery of waiting tables or making plastic chairs on an assembly line five days a week. For me, editing erotica has been just that sweet dream. But, my friends counter, you must get tired of it. It must get old after a while, they tell me. Even chocolate lovers, they're convinced, must grow to dread having to sample every morsel of roasted goodness that's shoved under their noses and feel forced to offer

an opinion on every truffle that crosses their palate whether they're in the mood or not.

Erotica, my concerned friends worry, must eventually become so tedious that it has the opposite of its intended effect. They ask me if I just can't stand to read about another seduction, if the idea of another first-time public sex encounter on the page is actually a turn-off. If reading all that erotica is actually ruining my sex life, or at the very least making me immune, or worse, numb. Desensitizing me to Eros.

It's true that I read—and after all these years, have read—an unbelievable amount of erotica. Like a good chocolate taster, I study when I'm off the clock. I read other people's erotica collections to stay current with the competition. I check out what new and seasoned authors are up to. I watch erotica trends with a keen eye (such as the latest craze, explicit romance novels).

I pay close attention to who's editing collections and how they're being treated by their publishers. The process is just as important to me: I found myself reading erotic anthology author and editor contracts for e-books that I had no intention of participating in, but wanted to know if everyone was being treated fairly and being paid the market rate (they weren't). I also read erotica written by friends to help them polish stories for publication in other books. When I get inspired, I read my favorite erotica stories aloud for my podcast, Open Source Sex.

On the clock, I edit at least two collections of erotica a year. Each one has around twenty stories in it. For award-winning, best-selling and prestigious *Best Women's Erotica,* I read every one of the more than three hundred story submissions I get a year for the book. I don't want a great story to slip through my grasp. And when my publisher tells me I have selected too many astoundingly hot stories for the book (as I did this year) and I have to let a couple of them go, turning down authors, I feel like I'm giving up a piece of gold. It's almost painful. I have an irrational need to see the hottest stories published, and I fight not to let go of even one gem.

Of course you must be wondering if it gets tiresome. You might be guessing that my sex life is suffering. On the contrary: I'm constantly inspired to try a new fantasy with a lover and often read the hottest gems out loud to the hot *pan au chocolate* that's in my bed, savoring the exclusivity of the experience—and always, the effect of the explicit storytelling. Let's just say it works.

But tiresome? Okay, I'll admit that I have experienced more than the safe human allowance for exposure to bad erotica. Sometimes, the writing is so bad and the scenarios so ridiculous that not only would no woman in her right mind believe the story itself, but I want to yell at the page or computer screen, "This is not 'Penthouse Letters'!" More than once, I have been just one "heaving bosom" or a "throbbing member" or "wanton love muscle" away from hitting "delete all" in my inbox and heading to Harlequin HQ with a pitchfork, a can of gasoline and a road flare.

Yet I am far from desensitized. If anything, I'm hypersensitive to the best that erotic writing has to offer. I can feel it in the first two paragraphs. I understand the life of the chocolate taster who can't get enough pure cacao, the sommelier who spends every weekend tasting for his private cellar.

It's when you know how something's supposed to taste, or in this case, the predictable arc of a story that includes sex, and you're surprised by an especially refined note (or moment) that turns the whole experience of tasting into feeling like you're trying a new flavor for the very first time. It happens in the best chocolate: a note of smokiness or a hint of citrus, a floral that changes the candy into a different experience by the end. It's not what it started out as; it's something more.

The stories in this year's *Best Women's Erotica* will show you exactly what I mean. Not a single one of them is what it seems, and each of them contains a surprise flavor that turns the experience on its head, while engaging you in a character's journey into a searing sexual encounter and turning you on at the same time. To borrow the phrase and tell you plainly why each story in this collection illustrates why I love my job: each one is better than chocolate. And each one is an explicit, erotic surprise.

In "Shoe Shine at Liverpool Street Station" by Scarlett French, one young woman's first time having her boots shined turns into a public sex encounter with a twist: sexual tension and release so contained that in the middle of a crowd, no one's the wiser. Louisa Harte's "Prime Suspect" is a superb piece of turnabout, where a female police officer turns a lineup exercise into erotic punishment (and pleasure), taking the upper hand with a macho braggart coworker, much to the satisfaction of both officers.

K. D. Grace's "Vegging" is a tense yet playful tale of a woman and vegetables, which seems like a stereotype, but this is no ordinary woman and the garden isn't hers: the narrative peaks with vegetable debauchery, thievery, the thrill of getting caught and a most unusual erotic punishment. Fantasy becomes reality in Loz McKeen's "Fuck the Fantasy," which moves from an ordinary day in martial arts training class to a hard-edged fuck where an instructor teaches a student a lesson he'll never forget, and we're treated to a two-man, one-woman bisexual threeway we won't soon forget, either.

Amazingly, Angela Caperton's "Timbre" is based on a real-life story where a girl working as an independent contractor doing transcription winds up with a hardcore BDSM scene to put into words; transcribing sounds, conversation, all noises in the room—she finds that the male dom not only turns her on, but brings her further into the action with every mysterious envelope she receives. Outrageous, hot and furtive are the best words to prepare you for Carrie Cannon's "Straight Laced." Here, we spend a moment in a lingerie shop where the horny female staff occasionally "model" for clients, culminating in a scene where the dressing room is a backdrop for a model and client tryst with an unexpected, lingerie-laden twist.

More mysterious envelopes and even more sexual surprises await in Heidi Champa's "Amy," in which a girl receives video DVDs by post made expressly for her voyeuristic pleasure: each video is yet another girl submitting to one man's rough pleasure and punishment in the exact place where our narrator once kneeled for the camera (and the man) herself. Set in Hollywood, Alison Tyler's masterful "In a Handbasket" delicately balances a small girl and a big man who turn longtime friendship into a deep challenge of belief and a hammering need for release, spun around the conflict of a lapsed Catholic. It's the kind of sex on paper that makes you flutter inside and sets your nerves on fire.

Anyone who's ever slept in a room where it seems your neighbors are only separated from you by cardboard will appreciate the imaginings that go on in Aimee Herman's "Thin Walls," where a girl listens, fantasizes and moans during the masturbatory sessions of her hot male neighbor, finishing off with a neighborly surprise. Giving in to the unexpected is the name of the game in Aimee Pearl's rough yet sweet "Where the Rubber Meets the Road," a high-fetish, public, seemingly endless sexual encounter taking place throughout a series of dates that begin at San Francisco's kinky Folsom Street Fair, blending dykes, femmes, bois and lots of rubber meeting the road (and silicone meeting every opening our submissive heroine possesses).

You can absolutely expect the unexpected in "On My Knees

in Barcelona" by Kristina Lloyd, in which a sweaty summer vacation evening in a Barcelona bar turns into a pay-for-play, slippery oral encounter, and the heroine surprises herself in how far she'll go with a strange man—and willingly pays a price for her own risk (and pleasure). And if you think you can predict what's going to happen in Amie M. Evans's "Man About Town," you've got another thing coming. Here, a straight boy who likes lesbian girls who like transmen finds himself masquerading as a drag king and falling for a femme lesbian who thinks he's a biological female—culminating in gender-bending sexual frustration bar none and a searing man-on-transman, gay male, bathroom oral-sex tryst like nothing you (or I) could have imagined.

Just when you think the sexual surprises couldn't get any more exciting or arousing, Anastasia Mavromatis's "Stripped" offers a complex story of sexual roles laid bare when a woman who comes from a strict Greek family with stricter marital traditions finds herself rooming with three men. If that wasn't taboo-breaking enough, the roommates unexpectedly strip down to one another emotionally, leading to a powerful multipartner sexual encounter where a lot more than clothing is stripped, and every moment of the revealings is deliciously savored. Lily Harlem's "Stable Manners" is a tightly written surprise of secret sex taken quickly and silently amidst the chaos of horseback riding instruction.

It's not riding gear that provides the surprise in Kay Jaybee's superb "Equipment," but the right set of tools for the job when a very big, tattooed, macho lover expects a night of tying up the damsel and instead finds the slowly savored, lovingly enforced view from the bottom—literally, his—to be just as satisfying. Taking us to the outer limits of the unexpected is skilled Sommer Marsden, who delivered a story that left my head spinning for days. "Still Life" is hot, explicit, arousing and very nasty in all the ways I require a story to be, but the process our narrator goes through to get off in her head and the physical enactment of her very unusual fetish will likely have you doing a double take as well.

Then there are the stories that catch you just slightly off guard but make you wish they'd come true, ASAP. Rachel Kramer Bussel's fantastic "Secret Service" is where "Kitchen Confidential" meets *Best Women's Erotica:* here, culinary arts meet oral sex in service to ladies who lunch, and then quite a bit more, when the owner of a very special New York restaurant tries a random taste (in a manner of speaking) of what's on the menu. Finally, bringing the fantasies nearer to reality is the book's closer and showstopper, "Shift Change" by Emerald, which makes sure that for us, a trip to Apple's Genius Bar will never, ever be the same. And the wait will seem just a little more endurable with the fragments of Emerald's multipartner story floating wishfully—and giddily—through our heads the next time we have to "take a number" to get a minute with a Genius.

I hope you find this year's collection as arousing, entertaining and truly surprising as I did—and as my lovers surely will, when I read them every unpredictable piece.

Violet Blue
San Francisco

SHOE SHINE AT LIVERPOOL STREET STATION

Scarlett French

Passing through Liverpool Street station on my way from the overland train to the Underground Tube, I caught sight of myself in a full-length mirror in a shop window display. Yeah, I thought, I was right to choose "smart casual" for today—the meeting was an important one but I knew that wearing a suit would feel overdone. The fitting black shirt, vintage glass beads, and green velvet A-line skirt were just right. And with my slightly-over-the-knee, leg-hugging, soft-as-butter black leather riding boots, there was no need for fussy, ugly panty hose. I smiled and walked on, feeling (mostly) confident that today was going to go well. And I had allowed plenty of time; I would arrive calm and have a few minutes to collect my thoughts beforehand.

I decided to grab a takeout latte before joining the madding crowd descending into the good old London Underground and veered off course to get a decent brew. As I approached my preferred coffee chain, well, coffee wagon more like, I passed a shoe shiner stationed beside a brick pillar. He was bent over, shining the shoes of a City Boy. The banker was reading a broadsheet, his arms splayed and his hands clenched, holding the pages open. As the shiner buffed the shoes vigorously, the man turned the pages in a studied fashion. He seemed to find the service uncomfortable somehow, a man at his feet working up a beading on the brow, in that way that some people who have a housecleaner feel guilty about it. Perhaps he used the paper to create distance between them. "Watch where you're going!" said an annoyed woman as she swerved around me, rushing toward the Tube. She was gone before I could apologize.

As I waited for my latte, I wondered what it would be like to have my shoes shined. My only knowledge of the profession had come from the characters of Dickens novels—consumptive children shining the shoes of the aristocracy and dreaming of a better life, boys who were the men of their households after Dad had been taken by illness or the drink. It seemed very different now—the shoe shiners were enterprising young men running their own businesses. Having seen the price board, it seemed to me that this guy could make more in a morning than I made all day. Still, there is something about feet and submission that lingers. I could think of several examples, including Jesus and the foot washing that so humbled his disciples.

As I headed back past the shoe shiner, sipping my latte, I paused. He was perched on his footstool awaiting his next customer and he looked up as I lingered. He wasn't at all my type—he was blond and square-jawed and his face had been somewhat scarred by the ravages of teenage acne. Yet there was something that made me look away shyly. I stared at my feet, noticing now that my boots were a bit scuffed around the edges. Given that they were my most prized footwear—and in an almost fetishistic way—I really ought to have taken better care of them.

"Can I help you?" he asked. His accent was a crisp Eastern European.

I looked up and answered, "Oh, ah, I have an interview. I mean, a sort-of interview. So I was thinking I should have my boots shined. How much do you charge for boots like this?"

"Well, yes, they are a bit taller than the usual boots I do for a fiver. But let's just say five pounds anyway."

Now that I'd been offered a deal I couldn't really walk away. And I had plenty of time to kill.

"All right, that's great. I haven't had my shoes shined before so you'll have to tell me what to do."

"Sit down in the chair here." I sat on the wooden foldout chair against the pillar. He swiveled around on his footstool to face me and moved his legs apart to fully straddle it. "Put your foot here," he said, indicating the rubber grip–covered footrest that protruded from his stool at a 45° downward angle. I placed my foot there and felt a little embarrassed—no, that's not it— aware that his crotch was literally an inch or two from the toe of my boot.

First, he used a spritz bottle to spray a fine mist onto the toe and around the sides where the sole meets the leather. He rubbed a cloth back and forth over these areas, presumably removing any dirt. I felt like I should say something.

"Are you Polish?" I asked.

"No," he answered. "Are you?"

"Oh, no, I'm from New Zealand originally." This city is such a mix that sometimes no one is really sure where anyone is from.

"I'm from Estonia," he said, as he picked up a blackened toothbrush with very worn bristles, applied shoe polish, and began to brush it over the toe and around the edges where he'd just cleaned with water.

"Tallinn City," he said. "It's the capital of Estonia. Have you been there?" I felt a tickling sensation across the bridge of my foot and in my toes every time he ran the brush over the top of my boot. A smile curled across my face, but I suppressed it; to my chagrin he looked up at that same moment and I thought he might have seen it, though if he had, he didn't let on.

"No, I haven't been there. But I've been to bits of Eastern Europe: I've visited Budapest and Prague. What's Tallinn City like?"

He put down the toothbrush, picked up a shoe brush and applied polish.

"It's wonderful," he said, as he began to run the brush over the foot of my boot in short, sharp movements. Something was happening to my foot, my leg and beyond. I shut my eyes for a moment. *Yes*, I thought, *it's wonderful all right.*

"It has big beaches and it is very picturesque. To me, it is the best place in the world to spend the summer."

The brush made its way up my leg, in those same short, sharp movements, causing a tingling as it went. As he neared my knee, the leather scrunched a little as he brushed downward. I suddenly felt his hand on my knee. My eyes flew open and I saw his hand, cradling my knee and holding the top of my boot.

"Is this okay?" he asked. "It's to keep it in place as I brush."

"Yes, yes, of course, that's fine," I said, noticing that a slight breathiness had entered my voice. His hand was warm on my knee and I felt his strength in the pressure he applied. He began to vary the stroke of the brush as it ran all the way up my boot, around behind my knee and back down again. He became sensuous in his ministrations with the brush. The closest experience I can liken it to is how lovers have licked my nipples—long sure rasps of the tongue, reaching the pinnacle and returning to the base to begin again. That's what he was doing with his brush.

As I glanced down, I noticed a swollen bulge in his jeans, straining against the seams, literally half an inch from my toe. Our eyes met and he said nothing, but he didn't look away either. I realized I was wet—and I realized I wanted to touch that bulge. Slowly, I inched my foot forward whilst holding his gaze. The edge of my toe made contact and I pressed, just a little, against the straining denim. His face didn't move a muscle but his body juddered noticeably. I looked up quickly to see if anyone had seen what was going on, but there was just a wall of commuters rushing to and fro, grim-faced and clutching their newspapers for the journey ahead. Not a single person made eye contact with me or appeared to notice that there was some public sex of a sort going on right beside them. It's funny how being in a huge crowd can have an air of privacy to it.

I turned back to the shoe shiner, who met my gaze and reached for his buffing rag. As if to dispel any thought that I may have been mistaken, he leaned forward to bring the rag around behind my leg and pressed his crotch firmly up against my boot-toe. He began to vigorously rub the cloth back and forth across the back of my boot, then round to the front, beginning at the bottom and working his way up. All the while, my toe banged repeatedly against his increasingly hard bulge. I closed my eyes again and imagined that he was just going to continue rubbing that cloth back and forth, up to the top of my boot, up to between my thighs...back and forth, rubbing. It didn't matter that logistically that would have been impossible; fantasy doesn't have to be encumbered with getting your legs in the right place, or whether you really could accommodate such an enormous cock....

"Okay, this one is done," said the shoe shiner, breaking my

reverie. I opened my eyes and slyly smiled. Again, he didn't crack a smile back—and the fact that his face remained serious made my pussy clutch and surge with desire. "Now, I'll have the other one," he said. I brought down my leg, which was encased in a boot so lustrous that I swore I could have seen my reflection in it, and replaced it with the other. I made sure to bump that bulge again as I positioned my foot. He shuddered again, much to my delight.

The shoe shiner held my leg around the calf. As he sprayed the water over the bridge of my foot, a droplet from the nozzle fell onto his fingers. He ran his thumb over his index and middle fingers in a way that caused a writhing in me. I imagined those fingers being plunged in to me, stroking me inside. Then I imagined them being withdrawn, glistening with my juices, and brought to his mouth. I could see him pushing them past his lips and sucking, to taste me. I was wet and open with want, and my legs involuntarily fell apart a little.

He kept looking up at me as he rubbed the cleaning rag over the water mist, then brushed polish around the sole-edge with his toothbrush, and finally began the shoe brush's ascent. With every long stroke of that brush, I imagined his cock—thick and uncut I suspected—pushing into me, filling me. With every slide back down of the brush I could feel his dick pulling out, to the very tip. Then, just as I felt on the verge of a whimper, he'd push that brush up my boot again and somehow at the same time be pushing that hot, thick cock deep into me. A sigh escaped my lips. His mouth curled upward, a smile finally, or perhaps an indication of triumph.

Bent over me, he kept up his brushing with effort until I heard a soft grunt. All that pressing against the bulge in his jeans...had he come—a small, tight orgasm in a confined space? I knew I was close and I had to come too. I began to think crazed thoughts:

maybe there's a hotel nearby; maybe there's a storeroom; surely there's a station bathroom for the disabled, big enough for two and with a sturdy lock? But I'd been to the toilets here—I knew the disabled loos were in single sex areas and there were attendants. Well, right then I didn't care if I got arrested—I wanted him to fuck me right there. With his fingers, with his cock—I didn't care. I looked around, scoping the station again. There was just no way we could do it without being seen.

I am not one for being teased; it just doesn't work on me. Rather than becoming horny, I just get pissed off or bored. And this was a tease, whether it was intended to be or not. But as I felt the powering down of the brushing after his burst of effort, it occurred to me that in all this desperation I was missing out on the moment. I hadn't expected to have an experience like this when I left the house this morning and maybe there was a lot more in store for today, if only I'd let it happen. I decided to let it; I made a concerted effort to relax back into the chair and try to roll with what was happening. Here, in the moment. Even if my pussy was on fire and I was desperate to come.

He stopped brushing and wiped his brow, that curled smile returning to his face. "Now, the final step," he said, picking up the buffing rag. I closed my eyes as his soft rag curled around my leg and was administered. I paid attention to the subtle sensations as the rubbing caused the leather to brush softly back and forth against my bare leg underneath. The shivers went up my leg and pooled in my cunt. I let them settle, an electric pond at my core; a tiny pond, yet full of waves.

As his buffing picked up speed, I allowed the swish of the cloth, the smell of the polish and the sound of his quickened breathing to join with the shivers from his ministrations. My body felt like it was singing, so intense was the experience. I continued to let it touch my senses as the shoe shiner began to slow, and brought the buffing to a close. I slowly opened my eyes. The station lights glared as my pupils adjusted. The shoe shiner smiled.

"I think you are satisfied, yes?" he said softly.

"Yes," I answered. I was thoughtful for a moment. Then, "I wasn't sure what to expect. But if this is what a shoe shine is like, it's no wonder you guys are so busy." I just know my eyes were sparkling as I said that.

"Well, some customers' footwear needs more attention than others," he said. Nice one, I thought. My boots hadn't been that scuffed.

Handing over the fiver felt slightly awkward, like I'd just paid for sex. But he smiled broadly at me now. "I hope you will have your boots shined again," he said.

I picked up my bag, and the now-lukewarm latte. "I'm sure I will," I replied, smiling back. As I walked away, the smile became a Cheshire Cat grin.

I was fizzing with sexual energy now, absolutely burning. As I joined the bustling crowd on Liverpool Street concourse, I contemplated going to the toilets and jerking off. I would plunge my fingers—four of them—into myself, whilst imagining him holding me hard against the door, plunging that cock I'd pictured right up to the hilt, thrusting hard into me while firmly gripping the back of my neck. I'd hear his grunts and feel his ragged breath in my ear. Relentless, he'd fuck me hard until I was finally tipped over the edge by the sound of his orgasm catching in his throat. And I would shake with relief, limp-legged, spasming against the toilet door.

But instead of continuing on toward the facilities, I turned in at the Tube entrance, the ping of unspent energy causing decisiveness in my step. On reflection, it occurred to me that the shoe shiner probably hadn't come, that at most some precum may have surged and been pressed immediately into his underwear (and the thought of this sent a further tremor through me). But it didn't matter either way.

When I finally nabbed a seat in the busy carriage, I closed my eyes and focused on the feelings in my body. I was aware of a contained energy that illuminated within me, body and soul. It didn't course through me or writhe around. It was, indeed...an illumination. Calmness descended over me, like the stillness at the eye of a storm. Perhaps this was what Tantric practitioners experienced. If it was, I could understand their commitment to it.

I arrived at the meeting on time and gloriously levelheaded. And when I crossed my legs as the meeting began, my boots shone in the light, a (wonderfully) teasing reminder of my morning's preparations.

PRIME SUSPECT

Louisa Harte

I sit behind the one-way mirror, tapping my feet. It's Friday afternoon at the station and things are pretty quiet. Some of the crew are out on a routine call, while the rest are busy setting things up for the after-work party. I'm looking forward to it; it'll give me a chance to socialize, to get to know my colleagues a bit better.

I run my fingers over my uniform, still trying to take it all in. "Officer Jess Roberts," I murmur to myself, enjoying the way the name sounds on my tongue: official and powerful.

The door opens. Carla, my superior, walks in and gives me a smile. "All set?" she asks.

"Sure." I open my notepad and take out a pen.

Carla sets down her coffee and pulls up a chair to sit beside me. She's been great, showing me around and giving me a feel for the place. Today she's offered to take me through the basics of a police lineup. Nothing formal, just a familiarization exercise.

"Okay, normally we round up a group of people who look

similar to the suspect," Carla explains. "But seeing as we're a bit short staffed today, I've just rounded up whoever was handy in the office to give you a feel for things."

I nod. So far, so good.

"We use an intercom system," Carla continues. She gestures to the microphone on the desk in front of us. "If we need to speak to anyone, we just flick this switch to toggle the mike on and off."

I nod, making notes on my pad.

"And this is a door lock for the room opposite," she says, pointing out the control.

"Sure," I say, scribbling more notes.

Carla takes a sip of her coffee. "Right, if you're ready, lets bring in the guys." She presses the button to unlock the door. The door in the room opposite opens and a troupe of six guys wander in holding numbers from one to six.

I run my gaze over their faces as they settle into line in front of us. Most of them I don't recognize. I've only been working here a few weeks and the department is huge. But then my gaze stops on Number Six. My brows furrow as I study him. With that sweep of dark hair and those hypnotic brown eyes, he looks familiar. Then it sinks in. It's Matt. The guy who's always making lewd comments about the size of my breasts or how my ass looks cute in my uniform. It wouldn't be so bad if I could think of a witty reply, but my throat always seems to dry up before I can answer.

I listen absently as Carla continues explaining things, my thoughts still focused on Matt. Only yesterday I heard him telling a colleague he thought I was uptight and needed "a good fucking." I should have belted him one, or at least reported him. But the weird thing is, his words actually aroused me. Not that I'd admit it. He's a really hot guy; women probably throw themselves at him. He doesn't need me to add to the crowd.

I stare at his haughty face through the mirror, reconsidering my decision. I still should have belted him one.

I drag my attention back to the task at hand. Carla asks each of the guys to step forward in turn, getting them to face us and then stand to the side. I watch their expressions, intrigued. Even though they know it's a drill, under our secret surveillance they start to look nervous, shuffling their feet and shifting their gazes like they're guilty as hell. Even Matt looks uneasy. I smile in satisfaction. It's a pleasant surprise to see him squirming for a change.

Carla's voice breaks into my thoughts. "So, how's that for a brief run-through?"

"Great," I say, forcing a smile. I can always grab the handbook later and swot up on anything I've missed.

Carla checks her watch. "Oh, hell! Is that the time! Look Jess, I'm sorry, but I've got to dash off to a meeting." She snatches her coffee off the desk. "You think you can dismiss the guys for me?" she asks.

"Sure," I murmur, my thoughts still consumed with Matt.

"Thanks." She heads for the door. "So for now you're the boss," she says, as she dashes out of the room.

The boss.

Carla's words reverberate in my mind. I set down my notepad and study Matt more closely. He definitely looks restless. No doubt he wants to get out of here to change for the party or rehearse his crappy chat-up lines to see how many women he can pull.

Well, he'll just have to wait. I've got other plans.

I lean over to the mike. It's still switched on. Good. "Number one..." I say.

Number One lifts his head, trying to place my voice.

"Number One, you are free to leave," I instruct him.

Number One nods to the others and strolls out of the room.

"Number Two, you are also free to go." One by one, I let the guys file out, until the room is empty. Except for Matt. Without waiting for my cue, he lays down his number and ambles toward the door.

I grip the mike. "Number Six!"

Matt jumps at the volume of my voice over the intercom. He turns to stare at the mirror as if trying to see who's behind it. Thankfully, my voice sounds different over the mike, stronger somehow. The anonymity and amplification mask my identity.

"Number Six, return to your position," I continue, trying to keep my voice steady.

Matt stuffs his hands into his trouser pockets, frowning as he strolls back to his place. He may not be happy, but for the moment, he's mine. And I plan to keep him here just long enough to make him sweat.

I lean back in the chair, casting my gaze over his body. I've never had a chance to check him out properly before. When we meet in the office, I always feel too awkward to hold his gaze. But here, behind the safety of the one-way mirror, I can check him out to my heart's content: the smooth line of his jaw, the full curve of his sensual red mouth and that fabulous physique.

Matt starts to edge toward the door.

"We're not done yet, Number Six," I scold.

"Number Six, Number Six," Matt mutters. "My name's Matt for god's sake."

"While you're in this room, you're Number Six," I reply, surprised at the authority in my voice. I'm even more surprised as Matt drops his head and scuffs his shoe against the ground like a chastised child. He lifts his head and squints up at the ceiling. "It's getting hot in here under these lights," he complains.

"Then take off your jacket," I say, impulsively.

Without a thought, Matt shrugs off his jacket, letting it fall to the floor.

My eyes glide over the broad line of his shoulders outlined through his crisp white shirt. Under the bright lights, the material looks almost transparent. Almost.

"Now take off the shirt." The words are out before I can stop them. I clap my hand to my mouth, holding my breath as I wait for him to bolt.

Only, he doesn't. Instead, his mouth opens as if he's about to say something, then closes as if he's thought the better of it. A mischievous look flickers in his eyes as he reaches for his buttons.

I clasp my hands over the mike, stifling a joyous chuckle. Jeez, he's actually doing as I say! But my laughter dies in my throat as he peels off his shirt to reveal his lean, rippled torso. Helplessly, my eyes follow the line of crisp dark curls on his chest down to the waistband of his trousers. I take in a breath. He's bloody gorgeous.

Tossing his shirt to the floor, Matt keeps his gaze level. His piercing brown eyes seem to penetrate the mirror. It's as if he's staring right at me.

I duck down, my heart pounding, worried he can see me. Then I shake my head, silently reprimanding myself. Of course he can't see me. Slowly I lift my head. Maintaining his gaze, Matt's eyes are strangely calm. Defiant.

I swallow, sitting upright in the chair. My move.

Summoning courage, I pick up the mike. "Now take off the pants." My voice sounds low and husky over the intercom.

Matt cocks his head, a wry smile spreading over his lips. He glances over to the door as if to check there's no one else lurking around.

"There's no one here. Only you and me," I whisper. My voice is becoming huskier. I sound like some horny phone-sex operator, working a client. Whatever I sound like, it's working. Matt tugs his belt from its loops and curls it in his hand. He cracks the belt like a whip in the air, before tossing it across the floor.

The sound makes me jump, and I start to feel a prickly burst of heat between my thighs. What the hell? I can't be getting turned on by this, surely. It's only a bit of revenge. Isn't it? I unfasten a few buttons on my top, feeling suddenly flustered.

Matt stands tall, his frame held high. Arrogant. As if he's waiting for my full attention before he continues to strip.

Well, he's got it. "Go on," I instruct him.

His smile broadens as he undoes his trousers, button by button like some teasing fucking stripper. We don't have long; the other officers will be back soon. Time to speed things up. "Hurry up!" I shout. A blush creeps over my cheeks at my impatience. I sound frenzied, like some crazy bitch at a strip joint, eager to see a pound of flesh.

Matt flinches at my tone, the smile on his face darkening. With a smoldering look in his eyes, he hooks his fingers in the top of his trousers and pushes them down to the floor. Stepping out of them, he kicks them away.

I set down the mike, staring at the hot seminaked guy before me. My eyes drink in the sight of him: his hard slender hips, his taut muscular thighs and particularly the huge bulge in the front of his boxer shorts. I draw in a breath. Is this turning him on? I press my thighs together, appalled and excited to feel my panties grow wet at the thought.

The room stills. Matt stands facing the mirror, while I sit on the other side, staring back at him, silence hanging between us. I can hear the sound of my heart pounding in my chest. This is it, the end of the line. It's as far as I should take things. But seeing

Matt's gorgeous body and that huge fucking erection tucked up in his boxers, I'm gripped by a need to see more.

"Take off the boxer shorts," I command. My voice echoes in the emptiness.

Matt opens his mouth slowly, his eyebrows raised. He tips his head as if he can't quite believe what he's hearing. "Ah, c'mon love, you've had your fun. Now it's time to stop."

That arrogant voice. Like he thinks I'm bluffing. Adrenaline pumps in my veins. "I'll tell you when to stop—*I said take off the boxer shorts!*" I even shock myself with my forceful insistence.

Matt hesitates, a look of surprise on his face. Then he scoops up his clothes and makes a run for the door.

But I move faster. Leaning over the desk, I flip the door switch. The door in the room opposite locks instantly.

"Hey!" Matt raises his hands in indignation. "You can't do that!"

"I just did," I reply. "You're getting out of here only when I say so," I murmur, enjoying my newfound power.

Matt wanders back into the room, looking contrite. He knows he's beaten. The crew will be back soon. He can't risk being found like this; he'll never hear the end of it. Following my orders is his only hope of escape. He lowers his clothes back down onto the floor.

"Now, the boxer shorts..." I prompt.

Matt swallows. Wiping the sweat from his forehead, he slowly pulls down his boxers.

I bite back a sigh of pleasure at the sight of his huge handsome cock. Jutting out from his thatch of pubic curls, it begs for attention. I find myself caressing the mike as if I'm stroking his dick. My voice drops in pitch as the words seem to come from nowhere. "Now work it," I order.

Matt starts to look nervous. "Are you crazy? I can't do that in here!" he protests.

"Fine," I say, still caressing the mike. "I've got all evening."

Matt swallows slowly. His hands flinch at his sides as if he's working out his options. Not many.

Seeing him vulnerable and exposed turns me on even more. "Come on," I purr. My voice is rough with lust; I barely recognize it.

Matt's cock lengthens at my sultry tone. I smile with delight, while he glares down at his throbbing dick like it's betraying him.

"I'm waiting…" I murmur.

Matt lowers his head. Slowly, he wraps his right hand around the glistening head of his cock.

Stifling a gasp, I press my hands to the mirror for a closer look. Oh, my god, he's doing it! He's actually going to jerk off in the station! Mouth hanging open, I watch mesmerized as he begins to slide his fist up and down his erection in slow lazy strokes.

I reach for the mike. "Not like that," I chastise.

Matt raises his head, questioningly.

"Do it like you mean it. Like you're at home, jacking off to some porn."

Matt glances around nervously. Pursing his lips, he lowers his head and curls his hand more firmly around his cock. I watch, riveted, as he begins to really work his dick, pumping his fist up and down in a regular, intense rhythm.

"That's more like it," I murmur. I squirm in my seat as my knickers grow wetter. I've never had a guy wank himself off in front of me before. I'm so close I can see the line of sweat on his forehead, hear his muted groans, feel his excitement.

Smell my own.

On the other side of the mirror, Matt's really getting into it.

Lost in his actions, his head is bent, his shoulders hunched as he works his hand brutally over his cock.

A knot of desire tightens in my stomach. Suddenly, it's no longer enough just to watch. Feeling my own need burning inside, I grope across the desk to switch off the mike. With an impatient shove, I push my chair away from the desk to give myself more room. Hiking my skirt up to my waist, I spread my legs and slide my hand into my knickers. They're soaking with arousal. Coating my finger with my juice, I begin to stroke my clit, watching through glazed eyes as Matt jerks himself off.

On the other side of the mirror, Matt's legs tremble and he staggers back against the wall for support, dropping his head and pumping himself faster. His lips part and he lets out an agonized groan.

Seeing him losing control makes me hotter. Excitement burns through me from my clit to the tip of my breasts. Stifling a moan, I spread my legs wider and work a finger into my pussy. With my other hand, I tug open my top to tease out a breast, pinching my nipple between my fingers as I watch him perform.

Through the mirror, Matt's eyes flicker closed. His thighs tighten as he works himself harder. It looks like he's close. I rub my finger furiously over my clit, trying to keep pace with him. As I'm pumping myself faster, pleasure builds like a huge wave inside me at his hot, horny show. The only sounds I can hear are my soft moans and the rustle of my hand as it works between my legs.

Suddenly, Matt groans and clutches the wall behind him. I watch transfixed as his body stiffens, his cock quivers and he shoots his load. At that very moment, his eyes flicker open as if timed to precision to meet my watchful gaze with a look so filthy, I can barely continue watching.

He never lost control. He had it all along.

That does it. The searing intent in his eyes sends me over the edge. With a final firm stroke over my clit, I join him. "Oh, god, yes!" I cry, spinning back in the chair as my orgasm rips through me.

Panting, I gaze up at the ceiling and take a few breaths. My heart feels like it's bursting out of my chest. My body's tingling; my hair's all mussed up. I lower my head to see Matt still standing there naked, his hands on his hips, his lips upturned into his trademark smile like nothing has happened. While I'm sitting here at this shabby desk with the knowledge I've brought myself off to this jumped-up creep!

"I take it I can go now...?" he asks, with a smirk.

The cheeky bastard.

Hastily tugging my skirt into place, I make a grab for the mike. "Yeah, you can go!" I shout, suddenly ashamed at my own slutty behavior.

Matt grins, leisurely pulling on his boxers, pants and shirt. Swinging his jacket over his shoulder, he strolls to the door. "Aren't you forgetting something?" he asks, patting the door.

I shake my head and jab at the button, unlocking the door.

"See you later, babe," he calls, letting the door swing closed behind him.

Staring into the empty room opposite, I button up my blouse wondering what the hell I've just done. As we fucked ourselves on opposite sides of the mirror, Matt did it with my full knowledge while I hid away, keeping my identity secret like a guilty schoolgirl with a pathetic crush. I scoop up my notepad and turn off the lights. Too late to worry now, I need to head up to the party.

Dashing into the locker room, I pull on my dress, tidy my hair and try to establish some decorum—hard when my knickers are still wet from Matt's show.

Smoothing down my dress, I push open the door and step into the party. It's already busy. There's a bar in the corner, fancy lighting and the strains of music playing in the background. I mingle with the officers, smiling and making polite small talk, when all I can think about is this afternoon.

Then I see Matt, standing at the bar and scanning the room like he's waiting for someone. Dressed down in jeans and a T-shirt, he still looks damn hot. My cheeks flush as I reenact that scene in my head. I duck my head and dip into the room, trying to avoid him.

But I'm too late. He sees me. "Hey, Jess!" he calls.

I turn around, keeping my poise, reminding myself that it wasn't me who was naked and exposed in the lineup room. This is my chance to wind him up for a change. As casually as I can manage, I stroll up to stand beside him.

"Nice dress," he says, running his gaze over my body.

"Thanks." He's not drawing me in that easily. "Did you have a good afternoon?" I ask innocently.

Matt arches a brow. "Yeah. Did you?"

"Not bad." I try to hide my surprise at his flippant reply.

"It sounded better than that to me," he murmurs.

I glance around nervously, my heart starting to pound. "I don't know what you're talking about."

"No. Sure you don't," he soothes. Then he whispers against my ear. "That bit at the end though. When you came." He lets out a low whistle. "You're a dark horse aren't you?"

My mouth falls open. "How the...?"

Matt leans in closer, his breath warm against my cheek. "There's a switch next to the mike," he says slowly. "I suppose it's easy to miss."

Oh, shit! I didn't switch the mike off properly. He heard everything.

"That doesn't prove it was me," I protest.

Matt chuckles softly. "Nah, but only a rookie would forget something like that."

If there was any doubt left, the hot flush spreading over my face confirms my guilt. I've been exposed. That's it; my reputation's ruined, my job's in the pan all because I had to get off! Matt's wisecracks are the last thing I need. I turn to walk away.

"Hey, wait!" Matt sounds insistent.

I turn to face him.

A dark look of hunger flickers in his eyes. "If it's any consolation, I thought you were hot."

I feel the muscles in my sex clench at his gaze. It's the same filthy look as before.

Matt steps closer, his lips barely an inch from mine. "I've not come that hard in years," he whispers.

A smile tugs at my lips. That's the closest to a compliment I've ever heard him give. Suddenly, I find the right words. "Listen, Matt. About that 'good fucking' you said I needed…"

Matt tips his head, looking faintly surprised.

I run my fingers down over his chest. "Meet me in the lineup room in five minutes."

This time it's his mouth left hanging open as I push past him to the door.

VEGGING

K. D. Grace

The fact that Todd Sheldon often worked his vegetable garden in nothing but minuscule running shorts definitely got Beth Gray's attention. From her kitchen window, she watched the interplay of hard muscle and organic greens as he caressed feathery leaves, pushing and parting, grasping the foliage then pulling in loving little tugs until the soft loam yielded up the perfect carrot, deliciously phallic and foppishly plumed in green fronds.

She caught her breath as he ran a fisted hand up and down the length of the shaft, rubbing off the remaining earth, stroking it as she would imagine he might his cock when he was hard and uncomfortable. The thought made the muscles below her belly tight and twitchy.

Todd repeated the act until he had four equally perfect carrots. Somewhere in the midst of watching his harvest, Beth's fingers slipped under her skirt, into her pout. She wondered what a carrot would feel like down there filling her warm, wet hole with veggie goodness.

The next evening she put on her sexiest sundress, took a nice bottle of Chilean merlot, and went to meet him. She'd moved into the house almost three weeks ago, and if she waited much longer, he might think her unneighborly.

There was no fence between their backyards. The real estate agent said neither Todd nor his previous neighbor liked obstructed views. After what Beth had seen with the carrots, she was inclined to agree. She walked across her yard and knocked on his back door.

There was no answer.

His car was in the driveway. She listened for the shower running or the TV blaring, but the house was dark and silent. She knocked once more and glanced around the vegetable garden, green and rank, smelling of heavy, hot summer. Her pussy twitched as her gaze came to rest on the row of carrots. Without taking her eyes off the magnificent foliage, she sat the bottle of wine down by the door, kicked off her sandals, and stepped barefooted into the crumbly warm soil.

Straddling the carrot row was an act that in itself seemed yummy and naughty, and squatting to caress the soft feathery leaves, even more so. Beth was surprised at the pungent scent released by her stroking, amazed that so much was hidden in the hole beneath that luscious foliage.

She could have sworn she felt a deep rhythmic thrumming pushing up through her feet all the way to her cunt. She could almost imagine the carrots straining beneath the ground in an effort to pull free, in an effort to get into her hand, into her mouth, into her pussy.

After a quick glance at Todd's back door for reassurance, she ran trembling fingers down the foliage as she had seen him do then tugged. Her heart hammered in her chest, her nipples drilled almost painfully into her sundress.

Nothing happened.

But she wasn't one to give up easily. She widened her stance, curled her toes hard into the ground and eased her hand down to where she could just see the intimation of orange mounding beneath the soil. Then she pulled, slowly, firmly, not wanting to tear the delicate foliage. Her efforts resulted in an olfactory banquet as the pungent smell of carrot leaves flooded her nostrils and the back of her throat, blending with the rising tide scent of her growing arousal.

Grudgingly the earth around the carrot gave. She could feel the yielding deep into the ground. When at last the carrot was free, she understood why. The veg she had chosen was obscenely huge, not pointed at the end, as Todd's had been, but comfortably rounded, a sight that made her pussy feel fat, swollen, hungry.

The carrot was conveniently free of dirt, almost as clean as the ones she purchased at the supermarket. She ran her hand along the length of it, wondering how the size of it compared to the man who had planted it as a tiny seed and lovingly tended it as it grew in his image. Was that it? She looked around at the rest of the garden. Even larger than the carrot were dozens of zucchinis peeking from under huge fan-shaped leaves amid pouting yellow blossoms. There were long, ridged cucumbers handing heavily from straining foliage that trailed off makeshift trellises. Todd's was a regular garden of phalluses varying in size and shape, and she had the overwhelming urge to try them all.

She planned to start with a lavishly plumed, delectably erect carrot. Brazenly she undid the buttons of the sundress to reveal the deep cleavage between breasts that fit a little too snuggly into the cupping bodice, breasts mounded high with just enough space to slide the carrot into the tight valley between. The pungent leaves tickled her nose as she wriggled and adjusted herself to the warm, slightly rough skin of the veg rubbing up and down, dispersing the droplets of perspiration now beading between her tits from the summer heat. Her nipples were achy and engorged against the heavy stippling of her areolas. She fantasized that it was Todd's cock between her breasts. One hand caressed and maneuvered the veg while she squatted deeper, pausing to yank the crotch of her panties aside. Her pussy tensed against the ticklish foliage over which she spread her juices with each shifting and grinding of her hips.

The world was hot, as though the sun were baking her from the inside out, as though the fondling of the veg had set off a chain reaction at her center. She pulled the carrot from between her breasts, glistening with her sweat, then wriggled and cupped herself free of the dress, running the foliage over her distended nipples, watching them stiffen even further with the tactile stimulation.

She thought about nearly naked Todd caressing his carrots. She wondered if he had been hard. She wondered if he resembled her carrot, or perhaps the zucchini straining toward her, growing from the plant like an anxious erection ready for penetration.

Impetuously, she ran her tongue along the underside of the carrot, tasting her sweat mixed with faint intimations of earth and the promise of fresh, slightly metallic veg. She swirled her tongue over the rounded tip fellating it as though it were Todd's cock, thick and ready to fill her pussy.

With saliva dripping down her chin from her efforts to deep-throat the carrot, she parted her cunt lips and thrust the veggie erection home, whimpering her pleasure, well anticipated, as her cunt grasped the shaft like a hungry infant at the breast.

One hand thrust the carrot in and out of her tight grip, the foliage slap-slapping the insides of her thighs with each thrust, while the other tweaked her clit until it felt bigger and harder than the stones lining Todd's outrageous, erotic garden.

If he had returned, she would never have noticed. If the entire five o'clock news team had shown up with cameras and sound crew, she wouldn't have noticed. Her whole world had shrunk to her pussy and what the amazing plumed carrot was doing to it. Amid the straining and the tweaking, she held her breath, held everything tightly stretched in anticipation, oh, so close, so ready, until at last the explosion rolled over her in waves, and she cried out and growled like an animal, losing her balance and falling backward on her ass in the middle of the carrot row.

With her pussy still thrumming from the aftershocks, she made an effort to clear away the evidence of her intrusion, feeling both naughty and slightly guilty, which made her feel even more naughty. The footprints she could wipe out easily enough, but the bent and broken foliage of the carrots where she had fallen, she could only hope Todd would blame on overzealous rabbits.

When she had done all she could, still clutching the pussy-flavored carrot tightly in her hand, she fled back to her house, to her bed where she made love to the veg of her choice twice more before collapsing into blissful, exhausted sleep.

She awoke in the early morning hours, the carrot still frond-deep in her cunt. As she wriggled around its delicious probing, she felt a twinge of guilt, and knew exactly what she needed to do to assuage it.

She slipped the carrot from her pussy, and the room was awash in the scent of sex and the veg that had pleasured her. She padded downstairs naked and lit the oven. In no time she hummed happily while mixing the ingredients—eggs, flour, lots of butter, cinnamon and sugar. When everything else was ready, she sat on the kitchen stool kneading her breasts and tweaking her nipples with flour-dusted hands until the stool was slick beneath her pout. Then she took the carrot, gave it a quick but thorough deep-throating, and thrust it into her wet cunt. Rocking and grunting and thinking of Todd, she enjoyed one last mind-blowing come before adding the final ingredient to the batter.

The next evening when she came home from work, she found her sandals neatly placed by her back door along with a shallow wicker basket mounded with small, jewel-bright tomatoes. Her delight over the tomatoes was tempered by the feeling that she had been caught in the act. Certainly Todd had to wonder at the coincidence of her strappy sandals on his back porch and his poor, wallowed carrots.

From where she stood at the window she could see Todd, in his usual skimpy gardening attire, hoeing weeds. She fumbled in the drawer and found the bird-watching binoculars her sister had forgotten when she helped her move in. Suddenly she had a close-up view of the play of muscles along his arms and shoulders as he pulled the hoe. She relished the way his buttocks in their revealing shorts tightened each time he struggled with a particularly tough weed. Then he turned his attention to the carrots, caressing the broken fronds, scratching his head and looking around for clues of what had happened. With the help of the binoculars, she got an enhanced view of his package, which bulged and rippled beneath the shorts just enough to make her fantasize about what he would be like when he was aroused.

Her clothes ended up in a heap on the kitchen floor, and she was well entertained watching Todd garden, while she sloppily ate tomatoes, letting the juice dribble onto her breasts and belly, watching him stroke and caress his vegetables. She wondered if he'd do the same to his cock when he was back inside his house. She wished desperately she could watch.

The last thing he did was weed the zucchini plant with its

beautiful zucchini penis straining upward toward his hand. She held her breath, fearing he would pick it, but he didn't. He only gave it a stroke, then turned back to the house.

In the morning, when she was sure Todd had left for work, she returned the basket generously laden with luscious, thickly iced carrot cake. She considered it payment in advance. As she sat the basket in front of his door, she gave the erect zucchini a knowing smile, and her pussy clenched at the thought of something so thick, so outrageous, fucking her. She tiptoed into the garden, carefully reaching out a hand to stroke the smooth green skin, now warming in the morning sun. A quick look around told her there were plenty of other zucchinis. Surely Todd wouldn't miss just one.

She was tempted to take it now, after all she had paid for it, sort of. But she needed to go to work, and somehow taking it home to the un-gardenlike environment of her house before they could get properly acquainted felt like having sex before the first date. She gave it one last fondle and rushed off to work.

It rained that evening. Beth watched in frustration as the rain battered the leaves of the zucchini plant. The only vegetables in her house were a head of romaine lettuce, well past its sell-by date, and a few shriveled potatoes.

How pathetic was it that she had planned her entire evening around a sexual encounter with a vegetable? She tried to occupy her time with other things. The kitchen needed cleaning, and the stack of junk mail that had accumulated like a growing avalanche on the kitchen counter needed sorting. But she couldn't keep her mind off Todd's phallic vegetables. Did Todd grow them because he liked them? What if she wasn't the only one using his garden to harvest sex toys? What if Todd liked it up the ass?

She could easily imagine him giving a carrot a good slick coating of saliva, easing the crotch of his shorts aside, then plunging it into his tight, protesting pucker. It might hurt a little, and he might shudder with the pain of it. But no doubt the pleasure would quickly overcome the pain. And his cock would get hard, so hard that the seams of the shorts would be stressed to the max, and he would be forced to slip them down over the half-dome muscles of his ass and shed them between the rows of vegetables. There he would stand, thrusting and tugging and grunting until he shot his viscous wad arching into the foliage and onto the soft loam.

That was it. Rain or not, she had to have the zucchini. A double check reassured her that Todd wasn't home. Quickly she slipped into a loose-fitting sundress and nothing else.

The rain was coming down in sheets, and dusk was just beginning to fall. The mud squish-squished between her toes, and she slipped and slid precariously down between the rows, nearly belly flopping in front of the zucchini plant, which seemed somehow taller, more intimidating in the rain. But the object of her affection was within her grasp, straining upward toward her hand.

Her clothes clung to her in the downpour, her breasts and her pubis and ass were well-defined in the clingy, nearly transparent dress. She grasped the zucchini as though it were Todd's erection, then with a gentle tug and a twist, she felt it come away from the plant, felt the heavy weight of it in her hand, the girth of it like an open challenge to her gushing slit.

The zucchini was wet with rain and cool enough to cause a sharp intake of breath as she lifted one leg onto the overturned wheelbarrow and spread her lips, not able to wait for veggie foreplay. She positioned herself in a half squat, shoved her wet dress aside, then grunted and pushed herself onto the unyielding vegetable, one painful centimeter at a time, whimpering as the zucchini stretched her protesting cunt, the pressure deliciously agonizing. She had never had anything so thick in her pussy before. She wasn't even sure she could accommodate such a stretch, but she squatted deeper in an effort to make more room.

The rain intensified and she stood in the mud wriggling and groaning her way onto the insistent zucchini, oblivious to the chill or the drenching, aware only of the fullness she felt pressing up into her, as though she had taken the whole of Todd's garden inside her stretched, aching pussy.

When she was fully impaled, she came quickly. Her whole body shuddered, then quaked, and she dropped to her knees trembling and gasping from the enormous effort to accommodate the zucchini, now firmly grasped in her pussy.

Before she could recover, she heard Todd's car pull into the drive. With her heart in her throat, she extracted her new best friend from her abused slit and made a dash across the yard to her house. But not before the heavy ridged cucumber caught her eye. And she knew she'd be back.

In the morning she woke stiff and sore from her night's pleasuring. She walked carefully about the kitchen preparing flour, eggs, cinnamon, sugar. Then she had one last ride on the zucchini before she made up the zucchini bread. When it was done, she slipped across the yard and left a fragrant, foil-wrapped loaf on Todd's porch.

All that day she tried to convince herself that she should wait awhile before she visited his garden again. After all, she had nearly gotten caught in the act with the zucchini. She told herself that if she let the anticipation titillate her, the pleasure would be even more intense. But she had never been much for delayed gratification. Besides she couldn't keep her mind off the lovely, engorged cucumber weighing down its vine, waiting for her. Anyway, what was one cucumber between good neighbors?

She waited impatiently all Saturday morning for Todd to leave the house. When she saw his car finally pull out of the driveway late in the afternoon, she wasted no time. Who knew how long he'd be away. It didn't matter. She was obsessed. She had to know what the cucumber felt like.

She threw on a loose minidress that buttoned down the front and barely covered her ass. Once in Todd's garden, she unbuttoned the top of the dress and slipped it off her shoulders until she could cup and caress her tits and tug at her nipples, all the while taking in the rank summer scent of things growing, a scent very similar to the smell of sex. Her pussy was slippery just from the thought of what she was about to do, and her swollen lips yielded to her probing fingers. As she admired the cucumber, her clit marbled in anticipation, and she gushed at the thought of what a bad girl she was. She slipped two, then three fingers into her grasping cunt, remembering the girth of the zucchini and figuring the cucumber was similar in size. This time she would not approach such a formidable vegetable without a little foreplay.

When she was ready and aching to be filled, she reached out a trembling hand for the cucumber, then winced and drew back quickly. The damn thing was rough, prickly, almost spiny. A little pain was one thing, but she hadn't anticipated this. She looked around at the carrots and zucchinis. Any other time they would have been perfect for her needs, but not now. She had her heart set on the cucumber.

"Well, this certainly explains a lot."

She yelped her surprise and turned to find Todd standing right behind her in his gardening attire, his arms folded across his bare chest, his gaze lingering over her exposed breasts and her hand still buried beneath her dress. She couldn't help noticing the way his shorts tented around a growing erection.

"The carrot cake, the zucchini bread, they were both delicious, but they were made from stolen veg, weren't they?" The fingers of his right hand tap-tapped against the bicep of his left arm. "I'm willing to bet you fucked my vegetables before you baked them, didn't you?"

She nodded from beneath a heavy blush. There was no use denying the obvious.

He clucked his tongue. "You're a very naughty girl." Without taking his eyes off her, he reached down and pulled up a slender carrot, then ran the foliage through the curved fingers of one hand, slowly shaking his head. Before she could attempt an apology, he stepped forward abruptly and brought the fronds down with a stinging whoosh across her erect nipples. She jumped and gasped. The pungent scent of carrot greens competed with the smell of her sex.

"Naughty girls, girls who fuck stolen vegetables, need to be punished. Bend over." He turned her around, and placed her hands on the upturned wheelbarrow for support, which forced her bottom into the air. Then he shoved her skirt up over her hips, lingering to caress her asscheeks and slide a solicitous thumb down the length of her cleft. Before she had time to fully appreciate his fondling, he brought the carrot fronds down with a brisk smack across her bottom, and she yelped.

"I'll teach you to fuck my vegetables without telling me." He brought down his makeshift whip again. This time she only moaned and wriggled her bottom, spreading her legs, wanting him to see what his punishment was doing to her drenched pout.

He couldn't help but notice how swollen and slippery she

was, and as he brought the fronds down again, he buried a finger in her cunt, then brought it to his lips, flicking his tongue like a cat lapping cream. "Mmm, I think I've discovered the secret ingredient to your delicious baked goods."

He smacked her one last time, then she heard him spit. She peeked over her shoulder to see him rubbing the carrot with his saliva, and without warning, he parted her stinging buttocks and eased the tip of the carrot into her puckering anus. "I picked this one a little too early," he said. "It needs to go back in the hole." With that he gave the probing carrot a shove.

She cried out in shock at the surprise invasion. The pain quickly transformed to pleasure intense enough to catapult her into orgasm as he thrust the vegetable in and out of her clenching anus.

He chuckled satisfaction. "I've never known anyone with such a unique appreciation for my garden, and I can make you appreciate it even more." He bent forward and nibbled her earlobe. "Don't move. I'll be right back."

He left her in an undignified position, bent over the upturned wheelbarrow with a carrot buried up her ass. But her need was so intense that dignity was the last thing on her mind. She tugged and tweaked her clit, dipping her fingers in and out of her still spasming gash.

He returned quickly and slapped her hands away. "Naughty little vegetable thieves don't get to play with their pussies. They have to make amends to the gardener." He fondled the foliage trailing from her asshole. "Besides, we both know you want more than fingers in your cunt. That's why you came to my garden."

She watched while he picked the heavy cucumber from its vine, oblivious to its rough surface. "Some vegetables need a little preparation before they're ready to be enjoyed." He rubbed off the spine-like protrusions with his thumb. Then he took a Swiss Army knife and methodically peeled back the skin, filling the air with the rainwater scent of cucumber. He peeled until the bare fruit was exposed all except for the bit in his hand, then he inspected his efforts. "There now, that should do the trick."

Her mouth watered at the sight, and her pussy tingled. She spread her legs in anticipation, clenching her asscheeks around her full anus.

He rubbed the cool wetness of the cucumber over her nipples, then suckled each of them in turn before he moved behind her. "You want my cucumber in your pussy, don't you?" He ran it down from just below her anus, over her parted lips and circled her straining clit.

She moaned and spread her legs farther.

"As bad as you are, I don't know if I should give you what you want." He circled her clit again and maneuvered the moist firm tip of the veg so it teased apart her lips, but didn't quite penetrate. Then he pulled it back, and when she struggled to push onto it, he smacked her bottom with the flat of his hand.

"Such a nasty girl."

"Please. Please put it in me." She rose on her toes until her calves burned in her effort to get closer to the tantalizing cucumber. The carrot foliage swished against her ass like a horse's tail, making her feel like a mare in heat desperate to be mounted.

"You must be so uncomfortable with your cunny all swollen and pouting. Poor dirty girl." He slipped the cucumber into her just enough for her pussy to grip at it, then withdrew it again.

"Please! I need it," she sobbed in frustration. "Oh, please put it in me."

Without another word, he shoved the cucumber home, and it was at least as big as the zucchini, stretching her pussy and lubricating her with its fragrant juices. Todd thrust both the carrot and the cucumber in rhythm until Beth was grinding and pushing back against him with all her might, growling and clawing at the wheelbarrow with each accelerating thrust.

In a frenzied move, he yanked the cucumber from her pussy, and her sex-crazed mind barely registered the tearing of a condom wrapper. "You need more than vegetables for a healthy diet."

She never saw his cock, but she sure as hell felt it as he shoved into her, manipulating the carrot as he did so. Suddenly she knew—cucumber or zucchini, there was no comparison to the real thing. His full balls slapped her ass with each thrust. He fondled her breasts, stroked her clit, cupped her pubis, then eased back, always keeping her just on the edge of orgasm, feeling full beyond full and ready to burst. As he hammered into her, his body felt as though it would shatter against her with the intensity of his own need, building and straining toward his release, until at last he grunted in her ear, "I can't hold back much longer."

"Then do it!" she hissed between clenched teeth.

He thrust until she thought he would split her in two, forcing the air from her lungs, causing joints to crack, and she rode him back, unrelenting until she felt his cock convulse. With a loud groan, he yanked the carrot from her anus, and orgasm juddered through her like an earthquake. She cried out and bucked back against him in a frenzy until he lost his balance and they both landed in the dirt, writhing on the ground between the carrots and the zucchini.

For a long time they didn't move; they just struggled to breathe, lying in the warm summer earth, covered in dirt and sweat and come; then he stood, took her hand and led her in to his shower.

As she soaped and caressed his cock, she observed he was

neither like a zucchini nor a carrot. More like a banana, actually.

He moaned his pleasure at her touch and curled his fingers
in her hair. "It's nice to finally find someone who appreciates a
good vegetable garden."

She smiled up at him. "I'm really glad to hear that, because
I'm counting on you to help me get my five-a-day." She rinsed
his cock, then knelt and took him into her mouth. Vegetables
were great, but it was exceptionally yummy to have meat on the
menu again.

FUCK THE FANTASY

Loz McKeen

The object of my fantasies for a good decade or so was Sean Burgen, though I only ever thought of him as Mr. Burgen. Mr. Burgen was a martial arts instructor and no pinup boy. No sir. But then, I never had shown interest in men who were "cute," or "hunky." When friends were plastering their walls with dimply little Corey Haim, I was perched on my windowsill, ogling the sunburnt laborer working on the house next door. When we were older, and the others were gurgling over Tom Cruise, it was Colonel Nathan Jessup that got my juices flowing. So naturally, the man who fueled and sustained my nightly fondling all through my teens and on into my twenties would have to be something special. And the eventual trigger, the event that finally dragged him from pure fingering fiction into red-hot real life, is definitely worth writing about.

It was all Marty's fault. The stupid bastard had hit me too hard, too often, and I was sick of it. I had put up with it for a while, but enough was enough. I was hanging around after class, and the minute the others were gone, I was going straight to the boss to dob.

Let me explain something. A good fighter doesn't need to hurt you to humble you. A good fighter will evade your kicks or brush them aside, and you wonder how it is that you finish the round in a lather of sweat and he is a picture of serenity. Marty and I and a core group of students had been training hard in the lead-up to the National Titles. Competition fighting is artificial. The aim is not to hurt or disable your opponent, but simply to score a point. Marty, on the other hand, was missing the point altogether. Not only was he attacking too hard, but he was defending too hard as well. My forearms and shins were multicolored from fending him off. The guy needed an attitude adjustment, and I knew just the man to give it to him.

I made my way to the front of the room where Mr. Burgen was packing up. I loved watching the back of him. His black instructor's belt pulled the jacket tight around his hips and the span of his back and shoulders branched out above.

"Hey, Cat. What're you still doin' here? Need a ride?"

"Nah. Thought I'd lost my keys." I held them up for him to see. "Actually, there was something I wanted to talk to you about."

"Oh, yeah. What's up?" Years of instructing and running the business had given Sean Burgen an easy manner. He had untied the belt and I could see the curve of hard, flat-packed muscle where the jacket gaped.

"It's Marty. He's still…" I searched for the right word.

"What…? Going a bit hard?"

"Yeah. Sort of. I mean, I can take it, but…" I sighed. God. How to say it without coming across as a total girl? It was crazy but, even after all these years, the guy still made me nervous.

"I could hit him back hard, but that's not the point. Lousy example for the juniors too."

He grunted and was quiet. "Well, sometimes, that's what it takes."

He leaned over and pulled up the leg of my uniform. There was a biggish lump down low that would be a bruise tomorrow, and some yellowing bruises higher up from last week.

"Don't you worry about it, okay?" He slung an arm around my shoulders and walked me to the door. He was still damp from training and I could feel the heat of him through my jacket. It was late and I was tired. When I first started with the club I only had school and training to worry about. Now I was training more, working fulltime to pay off my unit and studying as well. I leaned there against him feeling the bristly hair of his stubble against my forehead and the deep rumble of his voice in his chest.

"Marty's getting a little too cocky is all. It's probably time we knock him down a peg or two, eh?" And with that, he sent me on my way.

Two days later we were downstairs at Mr. Burgen's. He didn't mention our chat and I didn't see him talk to Marty during class, but it was obvious something was going on when they sparred together. I was busy with my partner, but I could hear the slap that comes from a foot connecting with its target, and the thud and hiss of breath that goes with a solid punch in the chest.

Others were looking too. Partners were still sparring half-heartedly but all eyes were on the young gun taking on the boss. We'd all seen it before and knew the ending, but that didn't dampen the shiver of excitement prickling along my spine.

Most of us had stopped sparring and had formed a rough circle around the two of them to watch. I turned just in time to

see Marty sink a corker into Mr. Burgen's thigh and then ram a
fist up under his ribs. Marty was going hard. His shoulder was
behind the punch and there was a meaty sound as it connected.
Mr. Burgen pulled Marty in close and seeing them there, pressed
up against each other, I wondered at the pure dumbness of men
and their hormones. Mr. Burgen's chest was almost twice as thick
as Marty's and as they turned, all I could see was Mr. Burgen's
back. Marty was lost somewhere inside the man's arms. There
was a hardness about Mr. Burgen that Marty would never have.
Marty was strong enough, for sure, and he had a tight little six-
pack under his uniform that would get him a contract modeling
for Bonds, but there was something about Mr. Burgen that said
he could weather Marty's storm and go on dishing it out. It was
there in his shoulders and in the calluses on his knuckles, but
also in his eyes and the set of his jaw.

Marty sagged as Mr. Burgen buried a big, gnarly fist in his
guts and I felt a tingle of fear. I wanted to see Marty go down,
but I didn't want him hurt. Mr. Burgen had his hip behind Marty
and looked set to take this one all the way to the ground, but
something changed his mind and he shoved Marty away and
clapped his hands. All over, everyone back on the floor.

We ran through warm-down and stretching and I wondered
what had happened. It looked to me like Marty was gagging
for a thrashing and Mr. Burgen didn't deliver. Marty was off
the hook before he was on it. I felt cheated. We lined up, and
after reminding us about the next training session, Mr. Burgen
dismissed the class. Our eyes connected for an instant and his
were cold and flat. Then he added lightly, as an afterthought,
"Oh, and Marty. Could you stay back a moment?"

It wasn't over after all. He just wanted to get rid of the spec-
tators.

* * *

"How you feeling? Good?" Mr. Burgen was back on the mat, smiling. With feet together, hands by his side, Mr. Burgen wordlessly maneuvered Marty back into position. Marty felt it and his eyes slid to the clock.

"Yeah. Um, fine but—"

"Good. Let's have another go at it then, shall we?" Mr. Burgen bowed, ready to begin, and Marty scrambled to catch up.

"Cat? Count us in." I gave the Korean command to begin and Mr. Burgen was straight onto him. Marty was jolted backward by a front kick to the guts and Mr. Burgen was there again, pounding into him with big, serious fists. Marty managed to dance away without going over but Mr. Burgen kept coming, working him toward a corner.

Usually, Mr. Burgen hung back when sparring with a student. He let the student come to him; he showed them what they were doing wrong and dropped them without hurting them, smooth and powerful, but gentle. That's why they call it a martial art. You got your arse kicked, sure, but he did it with such fluid grace that the landing was sweet and you'd swear he was laying you down to bed you.

All that was gone now. There was no grace about the way Mr. Burgen moved after Marty. He stood flat and moved steadily forward. He had forced Marty out of the square, but instead of backing off and letting him back in, he kept on at him, forcing him up against the weight benches. Marty was off balance and falling backward when Mr. Burgen grabbed him by the front of his jacket and hurled him back into the square. Marty tumbled, but fear had him up in a flash. Mr. Burgen closed the distance and caught Marty's retreating roundhouse under his arm. With one of Marty's legs clamped under his arm, it was easy for Mr. Burgen to sweep the other one from beneath him. Marty went down and cried out as all of Mr. Burgen's weight came down on top of him.

"Hurt?" Mr. Burgen growled in Marty's ear.

"No, just—"

Just winded, I think he was going to say, but he was cut off by Mr. Burgen's fist as it cracked across his jaw.

"What about now? How do you fuckin' like it, huh?"

Marty was pinned and bleeding and Mr. Burgen's sweat and spit rained down on him. Mr. Burgen shifted slightly and thrust his hips savagely into Marty's exposed groin.

"How d'you like that?"

"Fuck! What the hell was that?"

"That's my cock! C'n you feel it? That's my fucking cock. You're about to feel a whole lot more of it too, you little shit."

Now, most people would probably call time-out about now. But everything seemed fairly normal until Marty copped the backhander across the face. But even that wasn't so weird. Marty was a schmuck who needed a good smack in the mouth.

I was about to object, but stopped. A prickle of electricity had started flickering about in my chest when Mr. Burgen emptied the room. At some point, probably when Mr. Burgen ground his cock into Marty's groin, that flickeryness blew a fuse and was now pumping out some serious voltage down around panties level. Mr. Burgen was a thick, muscular man and I bet he had a thick, muscular cock to match. I'd been thinking about that cock a long time. I knew it, he knew it, and I'm pretty sure his wife knew it too, but that's where we left it, which is probably why I trained so hard, for so long, and got so damned good. All that raw sexual energy had to go somewhere.

The other thing that shut me up was the look in his eyes. And the stories. Fact: Mr. Burgen was a returned veteran. Hot rumor: Mr. Burgen was subsequently receiving a disability pension from the department of Veteran Affairs. That got me thinking.

Disability? No way. It's certainly not for anything physical. And there's what kept my mouth shut. The department doesn't give those pensions away. So, if there's nothing wrong with his body, then there must be something wrong with his head.

My first thought was to find help. Mr. Burgen was obviously having some sort of psycho-soldier flashback attack. Maybe Marty's bullying and my girly reluctance to fight back had resurrected the soldier's need to protect and defend. Although how all that amounted to Mr. Burgen thrusting after Marty with a hard-on, I couldn't fathom. I looked to the ceiling and listened for footsteps. Claudia, Mr. Burgen's wife, must have been upstairs somewhere. If it actually came down to it, and Mr. Burgen was serious about giving Marty a taste of his cock, then surely Marty would squeal. That was all he could do. Mr. Burgen was twice as big and twice as mean as Marty and me put together. Surely Claudia would hear the screams and investigate.

"She's not up there, Cat." Mr. Burgen was eye to eye with Marty and had pinned Marty's arms above his head. "She left. Three months ago. Said she always came second to students anyway so I wouldn't mind much."

He looked up at me. "Come over here. Sit." His voice was quiet now, the anger gone. His face was blank, detached. I wondered if maybe the fit was passing, so I went and kneeled on the mats near them. If we could just keep him calm maybe all this would pass without anyone getting hurt.

"Here, hold him." I moved closer so that Marty's head was between my thighs and carefully placed my knees on his forearms. That way, my hands were free should Mr. Burgen do anything crazy. Marty's hands were warm as he grasped my ankles. I beamed a reassuring smile down at him. The look I got back was upside down, but it wasn't barely controlled panic, as I expected. More like, barely controlled lust, which was just plain confusing. Marty wasn't the closet type. If anything, he was boringly straight. He trained hard and worked long hours. I was sure he did extra cardio work on top of Mr. Burgen's regular punishment. But then, after meeting his wife, I suspected that training was an escape from Mrs. Marty's reign of terror. Maybe too much work and not enough play made Marty a horny boy?

Mr. Burgen whipped the bottom half of Marty's uniform off, jocks and all, and my theory was confirmed. Marty's rigid cock sprung free and met his stomach with a meaty *thwack*. Marty's eyes flickered shut and he sucked in a breath. Mr. Burgen's eyes bored into mine as he undid his black instructor's belt. His pants were already on the floor next to Marty's but his cock was tenting the bottom of his jacket.

Fuck! What look was on my face? Was it stuck in a dumb stare, mouth slack, drool pooling? Because that's the track my brain was on. *Get it together, girl! Any second now he'll have the belt undone and the jacket off and then he'll be right here in front of you, all hot, hard flesh and rushing blood.*

Panic seized me. Pure selfishness it was, but what if the Real Mr. Burgen didn't cut the mustard? I'd spent years wondering, with fingers wandering. The Mr. Burgen I knew and loved was more than half fantasy. And my dedication to training was more than half dedication to Burgen-watching. What if doing this revealed him as just a normal guy?

I had seen the top half of him before, and it was definitely fantasy fodder. One of my best memories was of summer training sessions when he sparred in just pants and belt. The pants had settled down low on his hips and the belt had ridden high, framing that delicious overlap of belly muscle and hip. And the bottom half was fine too. Typical working man: hairy, sock-tanned, complete with chunky, wheelbarrow-pushin' grunt. But what about the bit in the middle?

"Martin is sorry for being a bully, Cat."

He still had his jacket on and was back kneeling between Marty's legs. Marty actually lifted his legs and placed them over Mr. Burgen's thighs. I couldn't see Burgen's cock for the fall of the jacket but knew that Marty could probably feel the heat and sway of it against his balls. Marty groaned loudly and I almost groaned with him as Burgen wrapped one of those big, callused hands around Marty's cock and started pumping it. The contrast of that massive, scarred weapon stroking the smooth, satiny skin of Marty's cock had me checking my pants. Surely the moisture was seeping through. And the gentleness with which he did it, almost lovingly: how could something so ugly, so purpose-built, still remember how to touch like that? My hand strayed to my cunt, ostensibly only to check for rising damp, but I kept it there. The pressure against my clit was delicious, and I couldn't help but give it a gentle rub through my pants.

"Martin wants to apologize, Cat." Mr. Burgen was focused on Marty's cock in his hand and his voice was a murmur.

"You should let him make it up to you." He saw my hand and a smile appeared as a crinkling around his eyes and a subtle lift in the corners of his mouth. He inhaled deeply through his nose and his gaze caught my eyes at the same time his nose caught my scent.

"Go on. Do it." His voice was guttural now; more breathy, more needy. The smile at the corners of his mouth grew a little.

"Drown the little fucker. You deserve it."

I stood and hooked my thumbs in the waistband of my pants. Marty was grinning up at me and winking, so in one smooth movement I dropped my pants, stepped out of them and sat on that stupid, grinning face. Marty's mouth latched like a sucker fish on to my clit and I gasped at the intensity of it. I ground my cunt into his face to try and force him to ease off a little, but he responded by plunging a thumb deep into my pussy. I sighed gratefully at the welcome intrusion and rocked back onto it. The vacuum seal on my clit had settled down to a deep, throbbing rhythm, and I could feel Marty's other thumb working the wetness back toward my arse.

I had shut my eyes when Marty first put tongue to clit but I was dragged back to reality by someone tugging on my belt. Mr. Burgen was there, but the jacket was off and he now had a firm hold on two cocks. I savored every sweet bulge and ripple as my gaze dropped from his wicked smirk down to the pair of slippery cocks thrusting gently into his fist. I saw the cause of the slipperiness. A big drop of precome oozed from Burgen's piss slit and slowly tracked down the purple, mushroom head of his cock to disappear underneath, swallowed up amidst the heat and friction of the two writhing cocks.

I didn't want to pity Marty, considering that I was sitting on his face and he was doing such a fine job down there, but lining the two of them up for judging like that was unfair. The difference in length was negligible, and difficult to estimate given their positions, but the difference in girth was brutal. Like its owner, Mr. Burgen's cock was big and mean looking, and I wanted it instantly. Burgen's fist, that looked so outlandishly large wrapped around Marty's cock, was now back in proportion. Everything was in proportion, and the fantasy was intact. My ability to think, however, was failing.

"Play fair, Cat. Jacket off."

He had my belt undone and getting the jacket off was no problem. They cross over in front, held in place by the belt and a little tie at the hip, but they always gape and come undone anyway. The bra was another story. Thumping someone is a high impact sport, so I always wore my firmest sports bra with the racer back, a bastard to undo. To complicate matters, Burgen had relinquished his grip on their cocks and, leaning forward, sucked half my left tit into his greedy mouth—bra and all. The other one wasn't missing out, his hand cupping and squeezing the nipple, but now I really needed the bra off. Maybe Marty sensed my distress, or maybe he missed Burgen's vise grip on his cock. Either way, he had my bra undone without missing a beat on my clit. The second the clasp was unhooked, Burgen had the bra up and over my head and was latched back on to my tit.

I looked down at him then, and before I could stop myself, I touched his face. Just for a second. I took in the rasp of the salt-and-pepper stubble against my palm. I felt the muscles in his jaw and throat working and saw those warm, brown eyes—Mr. Burgen's eyes now, not the blood-crazed soldier—swivel to look at me. I clamped mine shut and crushed his face against my boob and focused on the orgasm that was building in my cunt.

I wanted—no, needed—cock. Now. I was going to come soon and I wanted Burgen's cock in me when I did. But I also wanted to see Marty get what was coming to him. First things first.

With a sound like somebody opening an air lock, I disconnected from Marty's mouth and smirked up at Mr. Burgen. "Your turn."

I wasn't sure if he'd go for it but Marty didn't give him the chance to refuse. Marty took a hairy arsecheek in each hand and engulfed Mr. Burgen's cock in his hot, pouty mouth. I heard Mr. Burgen suck in a breath and he seemed to expand in front of me. Marty set a steady rhythm, easing off until the purple head of Mr. Burgen's cock almost escaped from his lips, then returning hungrily to bury his nose in the hair at the base of the shaft. At first Mr. Burgen seemed content to sit back and let Marty suck him. It wasn't long, however, before Mr. Burgen was thrusting gently to meet him. And not long after that, Mr. Burgen took a white-knuckled hold of Marty's head and began fucking Marty's mouth in earnest.

One of Marty's hands came snaking between my legs, searching for my clit, but I had beaten him to it. Two fingers dipped quickly into my dripping cunt before heading on to probe gently at my puckered arse. I was stuck staring at Mr. Burgen's veiny cock alternately disappearing and emerging again from Marty's accepting mouth. I had seen and felt enough in class over the years to know that Mr. Burgen harbored a healthy, hot-blooded libido. However, I was coming to understand that there were depths to the man that I hadn't even considered.

"Ohh, fuck!"

It was more of an exclamation than a request on my part. Marty had apparently tired of gently probing my butt, and had instead thrust a whole thumb and half his hand up there. But Mr. Burgen had interpreted it as an order to be carried out at once. He gestured that I should turn around and, popping his cock from Marty's lips, he took me by the hips and pulled me down onto his cock. He thrust hard to meet me and I grunted as my arse slammed up against the hardness of his belly. He pulled out and thrust all the way back in, filling me up and clutching me there, hard up against him. A few moments passed with jiggling backward and I half wondered what he was up to. I was so full and tight on his cock I didn't really care. Then he sank down carefully and I went with him, perched there on his lap, and I heard him groan loudly against my neck.

I couldn't see back there but judging by Marty's reaction under us, I could only draw one conclusion: Mr. Burgen had taken possession of Marty's cock in the only way he could.

He lifted me then. I felt the muscles in his chest and arms bunch and I rose up until just the head of his cock was inside me. Then, as I started my descent, he rose to meet me and his cock slammed home in my cunt. I looked over my shoulder then as his cock withdrew, and heard his sharp intake of breath as he lowered himself all the way down onto Marty's cock. It was too much. I almost came just thinking about it, that he was man enough to just take what he wanted instead of waiting around for someone to give it to him. He fucked us both then, just like that. He fucked us the same way he did everything: with a strong, smooth, inescapable power.

I went to work on my clit. My other hand sandwiched one of Mr. Burgen's sandpaper palms against my boob and urged it to be rougher. He ran with the idea and sank his teeth into my shoulder. Then with one final, savage thrust he ordered me to come and, ever the obedient student, I did. I ground down onto his thick cock as the contraction ripped up through my guts and found its way out my throat as a breathy groan. He held me there, spread painfully around his cock, and I thought for a second he had turned to stone. Everything about him went rock hard and tight and I felt sure one of us was going to tear something. Marty moaned and bucked underneath us and then with a grunt and a shudder, Mr. Burgen breathed again and I felt the weight of him sag against my back.

I leaned back against his chest until the last ripples subsided and my head lolled back against his shoulder. I could have stayed there for eternity, if it weren't for arthritis and shrapnel.

"Let me up, Cat. Bloody knees are killing me."

Well, a statement like that would never have made the cut in the fantasy screening, but the rest was saved in rich, vibrant detail and filed away for future reference. I still don't know if the psycho-soldier attack was real or just a scarily authentic fabrication designed solely to get into my pants. It doesn't matter either way.

It worked.

TIMBRE

Angela Caperton

Work. Thank all the gods and devils. The sound of someone else's problems would drown mine to silence.

I'd stopped by the post office that evening to get my mail: bank and credit card statements, worthless sales ads from stores I would never shop in, a sickly amusing promotion to reduce my mortgage payments, and two padded envelopes. Those were pay dirt.

I squinted to read the return address by the dull glow of the fairy lights strung up along the cockpit railing of the boat— which also served as my home. The first envelope came from M.V.—Chesapeake Bay. Max. Another surveillance tape, hopefully minus the loud cracking and popping from inside a nervous man's jacket pocket. My ears rang for two days after finishing Max's last transcription job. I shrugged and set it aside. Long or short, Max paid fast and well. If I finished the transcription by Thursday, I'd have money in the bank before the marina demanded my slip rental.

I lifted the other envelope and looked at the neat block printing of the return address. *R.K.*, and a post office box.

Port Orange, just twenty miles south.

Most of my in-state work came from Jacksonville or Tampa, the post office boxes not so discrete in hiding their federal court-house connections, and my fees deposited into my online account without a quibble confirmed my suspicions.

Port Orange. Local flavor. Maybe it would help snap me out of my funk.

A month earlier, the best relationship I ever had ended with a handshake, if you can believe it. I had stood in the cockpit of Aunt-Sea and watched Leonard walk up the dock to where his truck waited. My heart had ached when I looked at the little rental trailer hitched to the back of his F150. In spite of the friendly farewell, my heart sagged with guilt and loss. Why not? Leonard was a good man, strong and hardworking, with goals and ambitions that paved the path before him with perfect square bricks.

Maybe that was part of my problem with him—those square bricks. I liked sharp, unpredictable edges, different shapes, sizes, color. I wanted variety, to look beyond the blueprints and see possibilities, to glue chips of light and shadow fearlessly into a mosaic uniquely my own.

Leonard wanted a wife and home, maybe even children, although at my age conception and pregnancy would be an adventure of an entirely different sort. His fading patience at my lack of enthusiasm for even the most minor domestic trapping manifested itself in uncommon brooding and increased focus on his work.

For years we had been practically inseparable, our hands clasped, our lips locked, each body responding to little more than a look from the other. Just a week before the good-bye, we drank wine in the cockpit at sunset, staring at the brilliant oranges and reds of twilight reflecting off the bay, silent.

He'd asked me to go with him, to leave Aunt-Sea and move to New Orleans with him. They needed good carpenters with experience in restoring historical buildings and antiques. He'd talked about going there practically before the water had receded post-Katrina. He'd made the commitment, sold his home, packed up his possessions to start a new life—with or without me.

"Petra, come with me. You can do your work anywhere. Your brother's in Rotterdam, and your niece is a fucking junior at NYU. There's nothing here for you." This had gushed out of him after he told me he was leaving for New Orleans in less than a month. He didn't need to say more. I knew him well enough to know what had remained unspoken. He wanted me to marry him, fit those last bricks into the frame of his path.

And that part of me that loved him yearned to give in, and that part of me that had once given beyond reason stabbed me in the lungs and threatened my life if I did.

Survival instinct won.

So cradling Port Orange in my lap, I got comfortable in the cockpit of the fifty-two-foot ketch I'd bought after my father's death, and stared blindly at the deep reds and purples of sunset, drinking a bottle of cabernet I'd opened before the phone call. It had been a month since Leonard's departure. He called twice, once to tell me he'd arrived in N.O. in working order, and then two hours ago, his voice slightly stilted from alcohol—bourbon, I'd bet—the pauses between tight sentences painfully long. I knew my good-bye was the last I'd have to give.

I drained the last of the wine in a final numb gulp and tried to focus on the work the day's mail had brought me. My name, Petra Arin—Pete to my friends and regular customers—had become synonymous with fast, accurate transcription and confidentiality. What passed by my ears only went one place—the transcription file. It didn't hurt that I was also willing to work insane hours to get a job done fast. I didn't need to advertise. The Maxes of the world passed my name and website address around. I was known as a commodity who would transcribe wax discs if that's what had been the chosen recording media—and I didn't fuss as to the content. I could speak and write three foreign languages and could translate "fuck off" in six more. I've heard recorded conversations between criminal bosses and hired heat, and I have listened to the most intimate moments of more affairs than I can count. Authors and wannabes send me tapes and CDs of their masterpieces to turn their streams of consciousness into consumable structure.

I tore open the padded envelope and removed the CD and the folded stationery. Wine and curiosity had me wobbly-kneed on the stairs that lead from the cockpit into the main cabin of Aunt-Sea. In the galley I flipped on the light and unfolded the note.

Find enclosed a recording I would like transcribed. Please note all sounds heard, all conversation.

The rest of the letter contained the usual phrases and statements concerning payment, but I grinned when I saw R.K.'s assertion that he—the writing looked masculine—would pay me a 50 percent bonus when I finished.

The comforting creak of the boat wrapped around me as I weaved into the main salon that had become my office. Next to my laptop I snagged my portable CD player and headset and made my way back into the night-shrouded cockpit.

I settled on the thick cushions, put the CD into the player, the headset over my ears, and leaned back.

The electronic hiss of the recording device became the canvas. I heard a door open, footsteps, probably on stairs, one timid, halting, the other strong and confident. I closed my eyes, pushed away the slapping of the water against hulls and the familiar clank of rigging. The digital steps grew steadily louder and then, quiet as a whisper of summer breeze, a distant voice, the timbre deep, a depthless river of sound speaking two words that quivered in my belly and bolted fire to my center.

Follow me.

It was a command.

Every muscle in my body constricted as I listened. I turned up the volume and kept my eyes closed, trying to visualize what I heard. No mistaking the stairs, wooden ones, the tentative shuffle, the heavy fall. No sound but the footsteps filled my ears for what seemed an eternity. The man didn't speak again. Soon the sound of the stairs ended and more footfalls rang on tile or stone. Was it dark? It sounded dark, closed. I could hear the faint waves echo off walls.

Clicking. Some scuffs. Heels. The woman—wait, the second person—wore heels.

Do you trust me? A warm shiver slid down my back. How low could that voice go? It was like listening to expensive cognac, rich, hot, something to be sipped and savored, and that made my blood flow toward something I knew I wanted. I hit the rewind button and listened again. His voice wasn't free; it wasn't spoken into the air. He'd said those words with his lips pressed against flesh.

The pause gestated a moment then barely whispered, the shaking vibration of a woman's alto. *Yes.*

"Damn straight," I said aloud as I pulled my knees up to my chest, the crotch seam of my capris rubbing promisingly against my clit. I took one of the lounge pillows I kept in the cockpit into my lap and hugged it tight against my breasts, as if it could shield me from the arousal building inside me.

More sounds, like the friction of fabric, the rattle of what sounded like buckles, the uneven breathing of the woman, her deep inhalations accented occasionally by a sharp intake that oozed excitement.

I knew the sounds of sex. I'd listened to tapes of adulterous husbands and wives dozens of times, and transcribed three weeks' audio surveillance of a South Beach modeling agent who liked her girls tall, thin, and sexually open to her advances. My job allows me to be the ultimate audio voyeur, and while most times listening to sex can be tedious and exacting—I can only roll my eyes now when I hear a man yell "Oh, baby!" as he comes—once in a while, the tapes provide a few moments of aural foreplay and justification for me to unbury my vibrator and enjoy the ride.

How's that? Another shot of heat to my pussy.

The creamy purr from the woman had me biting my lower lip. I turned up the volume, as if more electronic hissing could open up the scene that I could almost see. I heard kisses—lip kisses with hard breathing between the soft smacks, and...

It was almost like the slow trickle of water, almost a dull tinkle, barely audible over the near panting of the kissing. I rewound the recording and listened carefully.

. Wet. Wet manipulations. Was he fucking her? Was that his cock sliding into her pussy? No. No rhythm, no sounds from him except his lips on hers.

She groaned, a short strain of throat to reveal her rising pleasure.

The sliding and slicking of flesh continued. Was he fingering her? Was he playing with her clit, teasing her pussy with long thick fingers, coating them in her succulence? I heard how wet she was, the sound unmistakable.

Her breathing became more ragged, more uneven. He was getting her off, and I'd squirmed my way into my little corner of the cockpit, my nipples sharp as barnacles. My own juices soaked my panties.

She's climbing, she's going to come.

Not yet.

My face turned hot as I echoed the woman's groan of frustration. The wet sounds ended, but I heard him touching her, the chime of his lips on her skin, but not her lips. Dear god, is he going to go down on her? I licked my dry lips in anticipation, straining to hear.

My finger rolled over the volume dial, turning up the sound again, eager to hear every gourmet sound.

WHAP!

The sound exploded in my ears as the feminine alto yelped in sharp response to the strike. I dropped the CD player in surprise at both the turn of the recording and the loudness created by my cranking the volume. My headphones followed the player to the floor of the cockpit.

Holy shit, what had I gotten into?

I picked up the equipment and stared at the player in my hands as if it were a sign of extraterrestrial life. I put the headphones back on and hit PLAY again, relieved when the CD cranked right up, starting with the entrance on the stairs.

I turned the volume back down and forwarded the recording.

Not yet.

WHAP!

The strike didn't sound like flesh on flesh. I've heard spanking before, and that isn't what it sounded like. I inched the volume up a little more, rewound and listened again.

WHAP!

It reminded me of something, the sudden dull edge to the contact with flesh.

Rewind.

WHAP!

Leather. Damn! He'd hit her with leather of some kind.

I pulled my legs tighter against my chest, my heart thundering.

More?

Yes, the woman gurgled, breathless.

I heard tapping, light at first, rhythmic, and the woman's whimper of desire. The tapping grew louder, the strikes a dull staccato, hide against hide. The sounds seemed to ebb and flow, the man's heavy footsteps moving back and forth, her sighs and groans stationary.

Was she on a bed? I didn't hear springs or even sheets rustling, but I did hear the ticks of straining material and occasionally, the high jingle of what sounded like buckles.

The tapping grew louder and stationary. He wasn't striking different places, but what seemed to be the same place.

The woman released a grinding moan and the tapping stopped.

WHAP!

Not yet.

The tapping strikes became less frequent, but more forceful, the woman's throaty cries riveting me, the man's deep, commanding voice bolting erotic lances through my cunt every time he spoke, every time he denied her. My fingernails cut into the material of the pillow. I was wickedly hot, the humid sea air beading on my upper lip, trickling down from under my breasts.

Then the strikes stopped and only the harsh breathing of the woman filled my ears.

I waited, holding my breath, stiff as stone and dazed. It sounded like cloth pulled over freshly sanded wood, smooth and warm. He was touching her once more. His kisses seemed tender as the woman's breathing turned into gulps of air. The wet manipulations began again.

I sensed straining again, and then the return of building cries. I could hear the fever in her tone, the unbearable pitch of her excitement, and I embraced the unseen woman's experience.

Open, he commanded, and the woman chuckled between the distinct sounds of licking. Footsteps away and he repeated the command to her, that single word drawing a pulse to my soggy slit. *Open.*

No sweet murmurs, no pillow talk, the man meant business and the woman liked it.

And I found, so did I.

Good. Where?

My ass, the woman begged.

I leaned forward in anticipation, hardly breathing as the woman groaned and laughed out a cry. What was up her ass? His cock, a dildo, a fucking banana?

The pulsing in my pussy increased, my sphincter clutched. I hadn't been this horny since before my marriage a million years ago.

Baritone: *Come when I say.*

The sound of flesh on flesh, the rhythm of fucking filled my ears, but the man with his gorgeous timbre didn't encourage, didn't howl or cheer on the conquest. Only his loud, ragged breathing gave any indication of his own exertion and excitement.

The woman began to keen, her pleas running over each other, begging, rattling the buckles.

Come.

The cry was shattering, a baying of release that vibrated through me to center in my cunt. Prolonged, the shout became a strangled gurgling, then a wheeze as she came down off Everest.

Him. What about him?

My hands trembled as I rewound the recording and listened again, desperate to filter out the woman's orgasmic flight, to hear him.

Just the slide and slap of flesh, the short bursts of breathing. No cry, no chortle or grunt.

The woman was reduced to whimpers.

Good girl.

The sound of light kisses, then buckles and the slip of material against material. His steps circled around the quietly panting woman.

THWACK!

Flesh on flesh, a hand on what was either a hip or an asscheek if I had to guess. The woman yelped, then gave a shaky purr.

Follow me, he ordered, his voice creamy and thick.

And the recording turned to static, finished.

Eight weeks later, I received another little package. *R.K. PO Box, Port Orange.* The pull tab on the soft-sided envelope never stood a chance.

I never expected to hear from R.K. again, thinking the recording was a playful gift between a couple, or possibly a blackmail scheme. Sealing up his recording and the transcription file in a padded envelope and dropping it in the mail was the hardest thing I'd done in many, many years. I don't keep copies of recordings, and I don't keep a copy of the transcripts on my local drive. Once I'm done I send a copy of the transcript to a data management service for back up, then put a copy on a CD or flash drive for the client. Then, the original transcript is wiped off my drive.

My gut ached for three days after mailing that envelope.

Now, my hands shook and the rip of arousal in my crotch

had my pussy on overdrive.

For two hours I listened again to the sounds of dominance, arousal, submission and apparently mind-blowing sex, but noticed immediately the woman was not the same sultry alto from the first transcription.

I didn't care. All that mattered was R.K., the maestro of the erotic symphony I listened to and put into words.

Follow me, were the first words he spoke, and my fantasies of doing just that raged for weeks after I'd finished the transcription and mailed it off.

Within three months, two more recordings arrived, each one hot as hell and intriguing, one with the alto, the other a new voice with a creamy Dutch accent that cried out her orgasms in old-world fashion. Each recording unfolded differently, including the alto begging R.K. to punish her and him doing just that—apparently by denying her the orgasm she so desperately wanted.

As I finger-fucked myself, I thought of her, and got off as if it could make up for what she'd been denied.

When the fourth envelope arrived, I was more than ready for the job, both monetarily and sexually. The five months that had passed since his last recording drove my imagination to all sorts of turns about where my favorite client had disappeared to. Maybe he was dead after tying up some drug lord's bored wife and fucking her brains out. Or arrested. If he was selling his services, the possibility that my sexy baritone was beating the ass of some jailhouse punk definitely fell within the realm of possibilities.

I glanced at his note, the form the same as all the others: get the sounds, bonus when finished, but this time he added a deadline. Four days. Like I would wait four fucking days.

I settled into the cockpit with a glass of wine and popped the CD into my player as had become my R.K. ritual. Listen, get off, transcribe. The muffled drone of music and partying reached me from different corners of the marina, the Friday night rituals of so many others taking a different course than my own. Headphones in place, it wasn't difficult for me to shove the outside world away and concentrate on him.

The recording started with the click of heels on tile.

Follow me.

Gush.

Six paces of his quiet footsteps and the click of heels. He stopped, the clicks a half beat behind him.

Kneel.

A brief scuffle of the heels, and then I heard R.K. moving, steady footsteps in the same area, then he stopped. A cloud of sound drifted through the air, maybe silk or satin falling onto the tile. I wheeled the volume on the player up, needing to hear, expecting the crack of leather at any moment, wanting that sharp blast in my ears to rocket hot sensation to my slick crotch.

A soft feminine sigh passed moist lips and the all too human static of hands upon skin filled my ears. A soft moan then a quick, excited suck of air. A dull tapping, maybe the toes of her shoes against the floor.

She whimpered, almost whined, then R.K.'s footsteps moved again. The jingle of chain and the sound of a buckle preceded the sultry murmur from the woman, a vibration that echoed in my chest.

Over.

The soft bump of movement, then the rain of metal on the tile. Footsteps, then a sound like the single snap of a flag in a breeze. The clarion yip of the woman made me chuckle, but mirth faded as she gasped, true alarm in her voice.

No, please. Her voice trembled, but no sounds of struggle or retreat accompanied her plea.

Shh, his depthless voice salved and smoothed. *Trust me.*

A stifled titter emanated from her, a long loud exhalation, then a rapid, but steady breathing.

Good. Low, rich and calm, he soothed and as he did, I squirmed, the thick blood in my pussy lips beginning to pulse.

My eyes closed as I listened to him stroking her skin, her rapid breath taking on the edge of climbing arousal.

When a high whirring was introduced, my eyes blinked back open. I rewound the recording and listened again. Vibrator?

The solitary whirr turned to a sweet hum as the sound was muffled by contact with flesh. The woman's gasps of pleasure confirmed my suspicion. My vibrator taught me that same language long ago.

Heavy footsteps and slight scuffs countered whining tonal scales as the device encountered different flesh. I heard the wicked rattle of plastic bumping teeth, a gurgled moan of desire, and the vibration of metal against the device.

He moved again, the high-pitched hum alternating between almost angry and muffled. Wetness filled my ear, the slippery sliding chime rising above the mechanical song. The panting of the woman rose in intensity, and I heard my own snorting in rhythm with the recording. The buzzing bounced one more time into my ear, then faded abruptly.

The woman's joyful shrieks filled my ears, *Yes, yes. YES!* Howling, then whimpering, her breathing broken of rhythm or pride, and then the golden meter of R.K.'s triumphant chuckle surged electricity through my body to jolt my weeping pussy.

Follow me, he commanded and the chain rattled, footsteps and shuffling followed, the accompanying harmony to the woman's orgasmic braying, her athletic puffing interrupted by sharp declarations of climax and the occasional sound of him slapping her flesh.

What the hell was he doing to her? They were moving, and from the direction of the sounds, it sounded like the woman was still on her knees, R.K. close to her, but upright.

My hips were moving against the pillow I'd pulled into my lap at some point during the recording. I wanted to come, needed to come. I needed R.K. to make me come.

Right, by god, now.

The sound of collapse filled my ears, followed by panting, shallow moans.

Good girl. Enough.

Damn! I held my breath waiting for the static hiss denoting the end of the recording. The wet spot in the crotch of my pants, the sweat on my face and the pulse that crashed through my veins demanded more!

His footsteps echoed on the tile.

The digital counter on the player told me there was more. I sped forward and stopped, rewound. Just his voice this time, the timbre as familiar as my own heartbeat now, intimate.

He spoke directly, unmistakably, his voice silk in my ear, my clit and tits aching already with what I knew lay ahead. The voice: *Petra Arin.*

Eighteen Juniper Street. Port Orange.
Follow me.

STRAIGHT LACED

Carrie Cannon

All of the women who worked at Jolie liked underwear. Why else would we agree to work for just over minimum wage plus commissions? But for me, the attraction went so much deeper I was ashamed to admit it to anyone but myself. There was something profound, transcendent even, about the structured femininity of a balcony bra, the earthy burlesque of red fishnets, and the wicked incongruity of industrial grommets straining against soft satin laces. With this job, I could finger tiny grosgrain bows and ruched mesh to my heart's content.

Every item of lingerie needed a body to breathe life into its limp, puckered frame, but once the body was there, I barely noticed it. The clinging lace, the winking Lurex, conspired against my concentration and drew me into a hazy wonderland of fabric-clad desire. As I helped customers in the fitting room, it was all I could do to remember myself and not run eager hands over their gorgeous taffeta- or shantung-swathed breasts.

On the few occasions when I managed to pull myself away

from fondling lingerie, my coworkers and I would indulge in a game of Name That Straight Guy. Straight men who came alone to the shop usually fell into one of four categories. The "blazers" stormed their way into the store, attacking the racks, and seizing the first item they found in the right size. *I do this every day,* they said by way of puffed chests and toothy grins. But the beads of sweat and the credit card already in hand belied their terror. "Cringers" were sullen and resentful. They made it clear they'd rather be chewing off a finger. Cringers winced as they handed over their requisite crumpled scrap of paper with neat, loopy handwriting listing sizes and preferences. The wandering, wide-eyed men with bemused faces and unfocused pupils were labeled "lost." They tended to be overly friendly and obsequiously grateful for any guidance.

The "dandies" were our favorites. They were perfectly tailored businessmen with Italian shoes who inspected each garter or demi like a market peach that might have hidden bruises. They spent loads of money, but you had to negotiate their dickering instincts and raging libidos to earn it. Usually, it was a dandy who would ask for modeling services. *I have to see it before I buy,* they would say, running greedy eyes up and down our figures. *I'm so sorry,* we'd reply, shaking our heads and summoning our best simpering, pouty frowns to show we knew how unfair, how terribly unreasonable, this policy was. Honestly, (conspiratorial nod) we'd be in there now, trying them on for you ourselves, but that big meanie in the office would fire us if she ever found out.

Sexual tension was our business, and we did work on commission.

Of course, there was no meanie in the office; the owner, Marta, was out on the floor most of the time, and she was more likely than any of us to break the no-modeling policy. On very rare occasions, a salesgirl might take a fancy to a customer—she might even indulge him in a clandestine modeling session in the cavernous dressing room we shared with the bridal shop next door, also owned by Marta. The room had mirrors lining three of the four walls and a raised pedestal in the center for a bride or pageant hopeful to admire her gown and have it hemmed. A folding screen politely hid the ladies from their attendant mothers and girlfriends while they changed.

Once dandies, or any other clients, were invited to observe a private fashion show, they became "larks." Larks were few and far between because none of us wanted the news of this special service to get out. I, myself, had never indulged a lark, and whether any of those private sessions might have progressed past a peep show, I couldn't say; I didn't ask. But I had my suspicions, given the large box of condoms Marta kept tucked away in the dressing room's tailoring cabinet.

The first time Marcus came into the store, he had the fresh, tousled look of an overaged frat boy: jeans slightly baggy, button-down tails hanging out, sleeves rolled just below the elbow. I wasn't normally attracted to scruffy types, but those pale gray eyes peeking out from dark, shaggy bangs sent a jolt of electricity slamming through me. I walked up behind him as he made his way slowly along the racks. Beneath the loose fabric of his shirt, I could just make out the exceptional geometry of his broad shoulders and thin waist, and I bit my lower lip in appreciation.

"Can I help you find something?" I asked. *Like me?*

He jumped and spun toward me; he looked like I'd just caught him shoplifting. His sheepish grin made my stomach puddle into my pelvis.

"Oh! No...uh...no...thank you, though."

"Well, don't hesitate to ask if you need help. I'll be over by the register." *Waiting for you to rip my clothes off.* Did I imagine his eyes holding mine just a little too long?

I joined Marta and Ellen at the edge of the counter. The three of us stood, heads crooked, almost touching, analyzing this, our only customer in the store.

"He's lost," said Marta. "Look at the way his eyes get all glazed over when he looks at the garters."

"No way, he's a cringer," said Ellen. He did look miserable. When his eyes weren't on the racks, they darted nervously from one side of the shop to another; he seemed to expect the mannequins to morph into people who would recognize him. When his eyes met mine, however, he didn't look quite so panicked; then he would blush, and rattle me with his self-conscious smile.

"I think he's cute," I said.

Marta glanced over at me. "Going on a lark, are we, Katie?"

I was busy noticing something very interesting—not about the customer exactly, but about the pieces he would stop and touch. They were all exquisite. His rough and tumble looks didn't fit the profile of a high-end aficionado, but without fail, his long slender fingers paused to stroke delicately embroidered Burano lace, or the impeccable engineering of a German corset.

"Maybe he's gay," said Ellen.

My heart dropped. *Of course, that explains it.*

"I don't think so," said Marta, squinting her eyes and shaking her head. She had a pretty good track record.

I had no good reason, but I didn't think he was gay either. My heart recovered slightly and a warm glow spread through my limbs. This was a man who knew an exceptional piece of lingerie when he saw it. And that ass… A twinge of disappointment reined in my excitement when I realized those fancy garments slung across his arm must be for someone.

As he walked up to the register with his bashful, happy smile focused on me, I resisted the temptation to throw myself across the counter, legs splayed, and beg for mercy.

"Lucky girl," I observed, running the scanner over the price tags.

"What? Oh...yeah." He looked perplexed, like he wanted to say something more, but his mouth snapped shut and his eyebrows burrowed into each other.

I glanced down at the sizes on the garments. I looked back up at him, eyes narrowing. Who was this girlfriend?

I swiped his debit card, making sure to take note of his name, and handed him the slip. As he leaned over to sign it, I had an uninterrupted view of his chest, straight down the front of his shirt.

That's when I slammed my hand down on his pen, rattling everything on the counter and startling both of us. He looked up at me, wide-eyed and questioning. I opened my mouth, but no words came out. *What are you doing, Katie?* He lowered his chin and saw the swagged opening of his collar. He stared back at me, slowly turning beet red. We stood like this, leaning intently toward each other, eyes locked, for what seemed like an eternity.

"You need..." I stammered, unable to make the words behave. His eyebrows lifted expectantly. He looked like he might start crying he was so embarrassed.

"You need to...see those on," I croaked.

"On?" He panicked, looking over at the amused faces of Ellen and Marta.

"I mean...on me. Yes. You should see them on me. Now."

He shot a furtive look over his shoulder, then turned back to me, leaning in even closer. He whispered, "Really?" The anxious mix of doubt and hope in his face made mush of my insides.

"Follow me." Feeling a little more sure of myself, I winked

at Marta's and Ellen's raised eyebrows and led my lark to the back of the store. As I approached the dressing room, the open doorway seemed to grow unnaturally large and the sight of it sapped my nerve. What were my plans, exactly, once I got to the other side? He still might be gay; he could have a girlfriend; I was only acting on a hunch. But my feet propelled me forward and through the door.

I heard the self-locking knob click behind us. There was only one way to find out where this was going, so I spun around to kiss him. Marcus must have had the same idea because his head was already in motion toward mine, and our foreheads cracked in a decidedly unsexy way. Fumbling and apologizing, he ran his soft hands over my forehead and down the sides of my face.

That was all the encouragement I needed. I started fumbling with his buttons, unable to wait another second, desperate to see what was behind his shirt. But Marcus grabbed my wrists in a panic.

"Whoa! Slow down. Can't we make out a little and, you know, get to know each other?"

This time my eyebrows were the ones to cross. "Sure. Then we'll crochet some doilies. Let me under that shirt."

Indecision clouded his face; I needed a clincher. My wrists still cuffed in his hands, I leaned forward and kissed his neck. Then I pressed my lips to his ear and whispered, "I'm wearing Chantal Thomass."

With a pained whimper, he released my hands. One long, panty-soaking kiss later he let me unbutton his shirt and slide it from his shoulders.

My jagged gasp made Marcus's eyebrows furrow together again, but he misunderstood my surprise; he was more beautiful than even I had imagined. Wrapped in an ivory jacquard, straight-neckline corset with a complex pattern of twisting leaves and vines, he was the haunting vision of perfection I'd only seen previously in guilty fantasies behind my own closed eyes. I pressed my hands onto his chest, trying not to pant quite so obviously. My palms moved slowly, firmly, down the steel boning and around his rib cage, lingering at the point where his ribs ended and his sides should have given way to soft abdomen, but instead retained their aggressive rigidity all the way to his hips.

Unbuttoning his jeans, I wrestled them down to his thighs as I sank to my knees and pressed my cheek into his smooth, firm stomach. I breathed in deeply, letting the heady scent of man and silk infiltrate my body and tickle all my private parts. The luxurious fabric surrounding him was cinched, tight and unyielding, but still felt liquid beneath my skin. I circled my arms around his waist to let the satin track of laces ripple beneath my fingers. When I pulled my head back, a dark circle of drool stained his stomach.

I lifted my eyes to his, beaming. The knot in his eyebrows was gone and relief flooded his face. Shoes and jeans kicked aside, he stood like a white angel in the center of the dressing room, with a host of angelic doubles spreading out to infinity around him in the mirrors. *Every one of them is going to be fucking me any minute now,* I thought, blushing at my own wickedness. His white stockings, clipped neatly in garters, curled and crimped the black hair beneath them. His raging erection strained against the thin fabric of his thong. He looked so sweet and vulnerable I wanted to eat him.

I stood up and ran my hands under my shirt to lift it over my head. The hoarse animal sound that gurgled from his chest at the sight of my coral-tulle-clad breasts made my pelvis lurch toward him. One of his hands pulled me close, his hot breath warming my neck, while the other traced the delicate, hand-gathered ruffle rimming the cups of my bra. "You are so beautiful," he breathed. I wasn't sure if he was talking to me or my bra, but I didn't care.

In a mad rush, he and I both pushed my slacks down and off so his hands could run unhindered over the mesh of my panties. He circled his palms over my ass and cradled my cheeks, feathery fingertips just teasing my creases. One hand wandered to my front and traced my clit. Electric shock waves shot through my body. He pressed more firmly, deeper between my legs, rubbing the thin fabric separating his fingers from my cunt. Almost in a swoon, I pushed into his hand, eager for the tickling half touch of his fingers through the holes in the mesh. He muffled a moan into my neck and I realized my panties were dripping. I pulled his waist closer and lost myself in a delirious haze of silk and boning against my bare stomach.

I'm not sure how I managed to pull away from him long enough to retrieve a condom from the tailoring box, but when I returned he was seated, leaning back on the center platform. He had pushed his thong aside to let his cock stand proud. I knelt down and stroked it, savoring the feel of his thin, slippery skin—softer and more supple than any fabric.

Before I slid the condom on, I straddled him and pressed his cock against my panties, pulsing my hips so he could feel the folded strips of mesh. His eyes were closed and his breaths were short, staccato rasps. With the ridges of crimped tulle dragging against my clit, I knew exactly how he felt.

It just seemed wrong for us to fuck with no underwear, so I pushed my soggy cotton crotch aside and fed his length into my body. Heat spread its creeping fingers from his cock out to the farthest reaches of my body. I was so giddy with the feel of him that I would have let my body swallow him whole if it could.

Rocking gently, with the satin of his thong chafing against the mesh of my panties, we fucked ourselves into a swirling oblivion of limbs and heat and silk. Oh, god, the silk. There were times I wasn't sure whether it was Marcus or his corset that was lifting me, shifting my position, consuming me with satin desire.

At one point I glanced up at the wall to see hundreds of startled, flushed women with their dark sweaty hair askew, staring wide-eyed and disoriented at me and each other. *That's fitting,* I thought vaguely as we all slipped back into our hazy joy—a joy that felt too immense to be contained in one single body.

Back in a straddle position, my pelvis began to tremble with an excitement of its own, separate and above our grinding hips. This expanding ball of energy pulled me from my reverie and my full attention turned to Marcus. I couldn't stop staring at him and he grinned back, looking slightly self-conscious. Suddenly, the corset didn't matter to me; all that mattered was the beautiful man in it.

With our fingers locked, I leaned down to touch his forehead to mine and let my body convulse in blissful, ecstatic spasms. His nails dug into the backs of my hands and a few minutes later his measured thrusts grew into a fierce hammering. I sat up and rode his shuddering pulses through to the last twinge.

Muscles twitching and chests heaving, we sat on the pedestal for several minutes while the wondrous surprise of finding each other soaked in. The clothes we had brought to "try on" lay in a heap on the floor, forgotten.

"That's going to have to be dry-cleaned," I said apologetically, touching the saturated hem of his corset. He grabbed my hand and squeezed it. I bit my lip and let my eyes wander nervously. "So, what are you doing next Tuesday? We have this shipment coming in from Milan...."

AMY

Heidi Champa

I turned the mailbox key expectantly. I always loved getting mail. The box was full, packed with bills and junk. It was amazing what had accumulated in three days. The brown padded envelope caught my eye as I sorted through my mail. It had been a while since one had made its way to my door. I could barely think as I ran my fingers over the scratchy brown paper. My pulse raced, my heart pounding like I had been running for hours. I felt like I couldn't catch my breath. I turned the envelope over and over in my hands. It was the same as all the others, no return address, my name scrawled in your thick black writing. I could almost picture you holding the marker in your hand, a smirk on your face as you wrote my address. I pulled the envelope open, and saw the plastic case inside. The DVD was blank except for the name *Amy,* in the same black marker as the envelope. Amy. There had been Beth, Tammie and Jane. Now, it was Amy. I fumbled slightly as I set the DVD on the tray of my machine, my throat tightening with expectation. My hands shook as I pressed

PLAY and the black of my television screen suddenly erupted into color. A young blonde came into view, the camera moving erratically at first, until it stopped suddenly on a close-up of her face.

There she was: Amy. A ball gag was stretching her mouth open, little trails of slobber running onto her chin. I could almost taste the rubber on my tongue, feel the harsh pinch of its latch behind my head. Amy's black mascara had started to run down her cheeks. Her big, blue eyes pleaded with the camera lens. She had the same look on her face as all the others. I knew it well. I had worn it myself many times. I couldn't see you, but I heard your voice, running through my speakers like honey. You were asking Amy if she was ready to take her punishment. Her nodding made her small breasts sway back and forth. I heard a chuckle from you; that satisfied laugh you had perfected long ago. I shifted in my seat, as I was already wet. Amy looked into the camera, lust and anxiety mixing in her eyes. Her small hands were tied to the foot of the bed, which was dressed in familiar-looking blue sheets. If I closed my eyes, I could still feel the sheets under my knees. She was in my favorite position, the one you put me in all the time: knees spread, ass high, my ultimate submissive pose. Now it was Amy's turn to submit to you.

I recognized the room as well as I would my own. I recalled the countless hours I spent there, in front of you, and the lens of your camera. I sometimes wondered how many DVDs of me were out there, being watched by other women. How many people have sat and watched you dominate and pleasure me? The thought of it made my pussy even wetter. As much as I secretly loved watching the DVDs, knowing *I* had been watched was even more intense. It was comforting to know I wasn't alone in my dependence on you. How many other girls are there in the world, watching another go through the same fate as them?

I heard your hand hit Amy square on the ass almost before I

saw it. Two more blows followed immediately, the sound echoing through the little room. Her cries died quickly behind the gag, a fresh batch of tears pricking the corners of her eyes. Despite her pain, I could tell there was pleasure there too. You asked her if she wanted more. When she didn't nod fast enough for you, you grabbed her blonde hair in your fist and asked again. She nodded fervently this time and was rewarded with two more hard smacks on her already red ass. This time, her muted moans gave her away. She loved it. She wanted to tell you so, but her voice was choked off. I could make out her teeth digging into the hard rubber between her dry lips. I knew the feeling well. I had done my fair share of biting my gag too. Suddenly the camera moved, showing me that you had two fingers teasing her cunt, trying to dampen the pain with pleasure. You fucked her slowly, but hard. If I tried, I could almost feel the rough texture of your skin sliding past my wet cunt lips, the way you would twist as you forced them deeper, pressing into my G-spot with ease. It had been too long since I'd felt you like that. I missed you, even though I didn't want to. Your hold on me was still powerful, even though it was no longer physical.

Amy must have been getting the same treatment from you, as her cries of pain had turned into muffled squeals and moans. I could hear how wet she was every time your fingers came out of her pussy. The wetness shone on your fingers, gleaming in the camera's spotlight. You got on your knees behind her and ran your tongue up the back of her thigh. Your pace increased, as did the moisture running out of her cunt. I saw her tremble, just as I did when you teased me that way. The whimper as you pulled your fingers from her was audible, even with the impediment. She was soon placated by your tongue on her cunt. I missed that sweet, salty tongue, the one that I had sucked on when I couldn't touch any other part of you. You dug into her ripe flesh, releasing another wash of juices from her cunt. You really had this one worked up. She wasn't indifferent like some others had been. Some of them had managed to stay so strong, trying to resist you. But not Amy. Was she as hot and wet as I used to be with you? I wanted to believe she wasn't. I still wanted to be your favorite, your perfect little submissive doll. But I knew I was no longer special to you.

You abruptly stopped what you were doing and the camera again focused on Amy's face. I heard you off camera, your tone harsh. Did she want to suck your cock? Did she want that gag out? She was nodding before you even finished the questions. She wanted you in her mouth, just like I had back then, back when you asked me the same questions. Your hand released the buckle behind her head. Amy sighed and cried all at once as the air hit her stretched, tired mouth.

Let me hear you say it. I spoke the words myself, in the privacy of my own living room: *I want to suck your cock.* I willed you to hear me through the television, to bring me back to you for one more chance.

God, your voice could unnerve anyone. She replied. Her voice was high pitched, squeaky. She wanted to suck your cock right now. Thankfully, you didn't let her talk anymore. The tip of your cock came into view. It looked just as I remembered it, thick and slightly purple. My breath caught in my throat. God, it made my mouth water just looking at it. I wondered if it felt the same to her as it had to me. Her cherry tongue rubbed against it, leaving a wet trail over the flesh I longed to taste again. You let her go on for a bit longer, but I knew what was coming. Before another swipe of Amy's amateur tongue was finished, you grabbed her head and forced the full length of your cock into her mouth. Her shock was overwhelmed by your insistence, and she had no choice but to take it. I could hear her gagging; I remembered the feeling well. Tears left her eyes in hot lines as your thick cock pushed into her throat again and again. The sounds of her moans were again muffled, and a little saliva started running down her chin. Soon, she had loosened up and was sucking as hard as you were fucking. God, you still had a way with women. You taught me how to deep-throat. Your new student was doing even better than I had. My jealousy shocked me and made me wetter.

Amy had her rhythm now and she appeared to be enjoying herself. You quickly put a stop to her pleasure with a hard pinch of her swinging nipple. She winced at the pressure and your cock left her mouth just in time for a shocked "Ouch!" to leave her mouth. You squeezed again, and twisted, just like I liked it. Amy didn't seem to like it as much as I had. I wondered if that was for me. I wondered if you still thought about me, about what I was willing to do for you. Everything you were doing to Amy, you had done to me. Things that I had loved and begged for, you were giving to her for me to see. You barely made her ask for anything. I had spent hours begging you, pleading with you for my release. I learned to love it, to need your permission. Even though I didn't need it anymore, I still wanted it. My hand was in my pants gently teasing my clit as I thought of the last time your fingers held my nipples like that.

Amy bit her lip to take the pain, until you eased up and gave her a break. Her nipple was hard and bright red when you let it go. Another yank on her hair, and her full lips managed a quick yelp before you covered her mouth with yours, sucking the air and what was left of her fight right out of her. As you sweetly stroked her nipple, she purred into your mouth, thrusting and wiggling her hips back into the air. I had never gotten a sweet kiss from you. You took my mouth like you took the rest of me, with force.

You want to get fucked, don't you? It was an absurd question, but one you asked without a hint of irony. Wasn't that why we were all there in the first place? But you asked, and we had to respond. She responded with the only answer that made any sense. So did I. We almost spoke in unison, choosing the same words to respond to you. Only she was the only one getting what she wanted.

Yes, fuck me please.

With her desperate plea, I knew you had hooked another one. One more soul who couldn't get enough of you, willing to let you document her pleasure and pain, as long as you gave her one more taste. One more earth-shattering, mind-erasing twist of pleasure from you. I had been replaced, just like she would be someday. But for now, Amy could feel the unabashed desire that forced her back into your room again and again. The searing heat of knowing you were there, ready to do your best and your worst. The giving up of dignity, of common sense, of time and space, just to feel your cock in her cunt until she couldn't think straight. I still wanted it, all of it. Maybe someday, when you tired of all of them, you would come back to me. It was my secret hope. But I knew my dream would never come to pass.

I envied Amy, just as I had all the others. I wanted to be her and hated her at the same time. The camera showed her face crumpled into a mass of relief and desire as you finally gave in and filled her cunt. The camera went back to its usual position watching your stiff cock enter and leave Amy's wet and waiting cunt, over and over. My fingers dove into my own empty, lonely cunt. I tried to remember the last time I was with you. The last time I got to be like Amy.

Was it really a year ago? A whole year since I cried out into the darkness of that room, just like Amy, begging for a hard, deep fucking. Needing you so bad that I was willing to let you tie me down, turn my ass bright red and keep my pain, fear and lust all on a convenient disk forever. It had been a long, long year. My desperate cunt craved, like Amy's, to be filled. There didn't seem to be a finger or dildo big enough to fill the void you left when you told me you were through with me.

You promised to keep in touch. The first DVD arrived months later. Another girl, another Amy on your bed, taking your cock deep inside her. Right now, Amy began begging you to fuck her faster, but your pace stayed steady and slow, teasing her with every swirl of your hips. My hatred for her grew as my pussy got wetter. I needed you again. I wanted you again, just like the last four times the DVDs invaded my life. You still managed to turn my life upside down, even though you wouldn't take my calls.

I'm going to come.

Her words made my heart sink but sent a rush of heat and wetness to my cunt. I knew better than anyone her need. You wouldn't make it easy for her. She didn't know it yet, but I did. I saw your cock leave her cunt, and I heard her moans turn to protests. My fingers transmitted her pain into my pleasure. Two more hard whacks on her ass rang out of my television speakers and went straight to my clit. That was what I wanted to hear. Her cries only made my orgasm bigger and better. My clit throbbed as my cunt tightened around my fingers, all while Amy lamented her current state.

By the time you were back in her cunt, fucking her into oblivion, I was lying back on my couch stroking myself to a second climax. I looked up just in time to see Amy's face twist into a knot and her cunt tighten around your cock. She wept as you made her come harder than she ever had before. She collapsed onto her stomach, her wrists rubbed raw by the scarf attaching her to the bed, the one I had given you so long ago.

Unlike on the other DVDs, this time you looked right into

the camera. Your eyes were looking straight at me. If I hadn't known better, I'd have thought you could see me right at that moment, my fingers wet from my own cunt, my body slowly returning to earth. But I did know better. You winked and the shot went to black. The familiar hiss of static filled the room. Finally, I pressed STOP.

IN A HANDBASKET

Alison Tyler

I think Prince said it best in "When Doves Cry." You know? Except in our case, people weren't digging the picture of Cal and me engaged in a kiss. They were digging, if you will, the vision of what we looked like in bed. That's what brought those evil smiles to their lips, the heady scarlet glow to their eyes. Strangers saw us, slight little me and big built Caleb, and instantly imagined us fucking. Caleb turning me topsy-turvy in his huge baseball-mitt hands. Me, on my knees, or on a step stool, sucking him off. Because I'm small, five four in my highest heels. And Caleb's huge, six eight when he slouches. I've got *angel* written all over my innocent features. He does double-duty for the devil with his shaved head and a barrel chest, muscles on his muscles.

Of course, there's more.

More to make people's heads turn when we stride by.

You see, we're an interracial couple, the two of us. I'm not only white, but that whiter-shade-of-pale type of white. I can get a third-degree burn by looking at travel websites. Cal's darkness seems to emphasize how fair I am, or my translucent complexion gives more polished depth to his.

We were friends, though, just friends; not "friends with benefits," not friends who fuck. We were friends who could drink together, sure, talk about anything, smoke a little pot when one of us was lucky enough to score a joint. Why weren't we making the beast with two backs, as Iago says, late at night, when nobody else was around? Because at least one of us always had someone steady, to sweep those dirty thoughts under the sofa of his or her mind.

Friends we were, and I was sure that's all we ever would be, until I moved to L.A., and he decided to come visit one weekend. For the first time ever, we found ourselves single at the same time. Did Cal realize that when he hugged me at the airport, when he lifted me clear off the ground in his warm embrace so that my cork-soled espadrilles kicked up behind me? Or did those thoughts come later, put in our heads by other dirty-minded people?

From the moment we walked out of the airport together into the heat-crimped Southern-California-in-the-summertime air, I began noticing the looks. I'd never really been aware before of people giving us the evil eye; we'd usually hung out with a group. Now, everywhere we went, people looked at us.

"Is it you?" I asked him, because he is so intensely tall.

"It's us," he said quietly, patiently. Always patient, that's Cal.

"What do you mean?"

"What do you think, chicklet. What do you think they're thinking?"

I didn't answer that. But when I let my gaze fall on him, I started to, well, dig the picture. I started to imagine his hands on me—those big, palm-a-basketball hands. Fuck the step stool, I saw me on the edge of the bed, ruby-glossed lips parted,

mouth open and hungry, waiting for the very first taste.

Clearly, I wasn't alone.

After dropping off his suitcase, I took Caleb out for a walk in my favorite neighborhood in Hollywood, an area where anything is possible. Strolling down the street, you'll pass happy-go-lucky transvestites, and young male prostitutes, and women who are so goddamn gorgeous you have no idea they have a dick between their legs until you get them home. And by that point, you just won't care.

Still, when Caleb reached for my hand, we drew our own share of immediate gawkers. Heads turned. Jaws dropped.

I suppose that's why the street preacher chose us to holler at from his pulpit on Sunset Boulevard. "Sinners!" he shouted. "You're going to hell!"

Now, I wouldn't shout anything at Caleb. I mean, the man could bench-press four of me. But this Bible-thumper had his book in hand, and he began to target us specifically. Caleb started laughing. He made me wait with him, while the geeky religious zealot quoted inane Biblical passages at us, until finally, I tugged at Cal's wrist, demanding we move on. Yet my mind stayed back in that makeshift pulpit. I couldn't understand.

"You're going to hell!" the man shrieked in our wake.

Were we going there because we were friends? Or because Caleb was black and I was white? Or because the preacher, like everyone else, imagined what we might look like in bed, Caleb bending me over the mattress and fucking the living shit out of me. How could I take all of him? If he were hung to match his size, his cock would be as long as my forearm.

"Why do you think we're going to hell?" I asked innocently as we walked away.

"It might have something to do with your shirt," Caleb said, kindly.

I looked down. I was wearing one of my favorite tees. I'd forgotten completely. The tight-fitting baby-doll white one with SINNER in bold red across my small breasts.

"But you're not wearing a SINNER shirt," I pointed out.

Caleb grinned at me. "Wouldn't fit."

"What fellowship hath light with darkness?" the preacher's voice sailed after us.

"I was wondering when he'd get there," Caleb sighed. I looked up at him, as I always was doing. Up and up and up. "You know, 2 Corinthians has got fuck all to do with interracial relationships. It's about believers and nonbelievers."

My eyes widened. "Which are you?" Religion had never come up with us before. We'd talked politics. We'd talked favorite TV shows from the '80s. And which band was better, Parliament or Three Dog Night. But religion? Not on our agenda, until he said the words:

"A believer."

I swallowed hard, but then Caleb turned me around so that I could see our reflection in the window of Vagrants.

"You can't be a lapsed Catholic without first being a practicing Catholic. I know my Scripture."

"But you said—"

"Now, I'm a believer in what you and I could do together."

"Do?" my heart hammered in my chest.

"You know..." he said, his big hands tracing my shoulders, then down to my arms, so that his flesh touched mine. "What fellowship hath light with darkness?" he murmured in my ear. We looked good together. No doubt about it. And I was wet, at his touch and at his words.

Once again, I thought I understood. Not why we were going to hell, but why we were getting those looks. Because it was difficult to look at us and not imagine how we might fuck, how

Caleb might toss me up in the air, or pin me against the wall, like a butterfly for his collection. From the expression on Caleb's face, he seemed to be thinking the exact same thing.

"We could make it work," he said, and his huge hands wandered over my chest, thumb tracing the letters. Slow on the S-I-N, making my nipples harden instantly.

"I've always been with tall guys," I told him, with as much cold seriousness as if that were a confession I should make on my knees, perhaps as a way to let him know I agreed. We could make it work. Still I'd never been with anyone as big as Caleb.

"When you're lying down, height doesn't matter," he teased.

But we weren't going to be lying down, were we? That wouldn't be any fun at all. Caleb was going to hold me up and fuck me. He was going to turn me upside down and drive his cock into my mouth. I weighed nothing compared to what he was accustomed to hefting.

We barely made it home, back to my apartment by the beach, where he stripped off my SINENR shirt to have at my naked breasts; his mouth, warm on my nipples, first the left then the right; his huge hands on my red-and-white floral skirt, yanking the fabric down my thighs, waiting for me to kick the bit of summery fluff aside. Not quite so patient now, was Cal. Not quite so easygoing. He was on a mission—different from the one of the street preacher. He was on a mission to get into me, deep, his tongue on my pussy, hands parting my ass while he sucked my clit.

The heat surrounded us: Santa Monica in the summertime, melting popsicles and no lights on; that electric smell of hot asphalt and salt breezes. And Cal's mouth working me, tongue ringing my clit, those warm strong hands opening me up now, drumming, strumming in a heady rhythm along the crack of my ass.

"You said you were a believer," I remembered suddenly, gazing down into his coffee-brown eyes, seeing the humor that I always saw when he looked at me—realizing in a flash it was because this was the first time I'd ever looked down at him, first time I was ever above.

But then he hoisted me up, lifting me in his arms so I had to put my hands on his shoulders to steady myself, feeling his muscles through his sweat-dampened T-shirt. I could have put my palms up flat on the ceiling if I'd wanted to. Instead, I gripped into his arms, knowing he was going to rip my panties aside any moment. Knowing that we were going to—what was it?

"Fellowship of light with darkness," Cal murmured, letting me feel the head of his cock at the split of my lips. Letting me steel myself now for the first taste of him.

"Does *fellowship* mean fuck?" I asked innocently.

"Only someone who wears the word *sinner* on her chest would ask a question like that," Cal teased. And then he got quiet, because he'd felt me squeeze him. Tight. Once and then release. He responded by plunging forward, driving firmly inside of me. And sweet Jesus, right then I started to think I might become a believer for real.

A believer in me and Caleb.

Forget Cain. We were able. Able to fuck like a dream. His hands moving, holding, lifting me so that I felt weightless, as if we were fucking in water, fucking in heat that's both breathable and surrounding. Flames licking our skin. The sound of fire crackling.

Caleb's strong, hard body pinned me to the wall, held me firmly then brought me down over and over on the length of his shaft. The pleasure floored me. Or lifted me up. I couldn't comprehend the sweetness, sparked with pain from his size, from the way that he stretched me. I'd heard of being fucked hard, fucked until you could feel that cock hammering against the back of your throat. But I never had that feeling until Caleb brought me to the bed, set me down and got behind me.

Here we were, bringing that picture to life, becoming the image that all of those dirty-minded people pictured when they saw us walking, when they saw two friends together. This was the culmination of all of those stares. And they were right, those filthy-thinking people. Being fucked by Caleb was transcendent, shattering in that way that makes you flutter inside, every nerve ending alive—every fiber on fire.

Caleb gripped my hair in one fist and pulled as he fucked me, as he sealed himself into me, whispering sweet words the whole time. Not Scripture, but promises, or rather confessions: How he'd wanted to do this from the start. How he was one of those dirty-minded people who imagined what I'd look like naked whenever he saw me.

"Like a sinner?" I whispered.

"We're all sinners," he sighed, as he came.

I slid one hand on top of his, pumping against my clit, showing him the way to take me there, letting his finger do the trick, so that I climaxed right after him, melting with him into the heat.

But he recovered quicker than I did, gripping me into his arms, holding me against him as the breeze barely stirred my lacy curtains.

"You know," I told him, turning to look into his eyes, "we're going to hell."

He laughed, that rumbling baritone laugh that I've always loved. "At least, chicklet, we'll be there together."

THIN WALLS

Aimee Herman

I can hear the sounds of him fucking himself from the shared wall between my bathroom and his. I have no idea what he looks like. I imagine a big, burly man with chest hair, back hair, and a thick mass of dark curls across his head. His grunts are muffled, but I can still sense the depth of his voice.

The bathroom isn't very big—not much space to walk around, though I can't imagine he needs to walk around during this self-service moment. No, he's probably in front of the toilet, lid up, so he can easily shoot his wad into the pond of recycled water for easier cleanup. Or he could be in the bathtub, finishing up his shower by finishing up himself.

He lives in the apartment right next door. In the eight months that I've lived here, we've never seen each other's face. The sound of him masturbating has become regular, almost like clockwork. He's a man of endurance, fucking himself at least six times a week. I assume it's solo, as I've never heard another voice accompanying his.

In my head, I have already named him: Lionel Enthusiast III. I imagine he works by day as a short-order cook at the nearby pancake house. I envision him having to excuse himself every few hours to tug himself toward ejaculation. Maybe he has an accomplice, a young waitress with a blue apron tied tightly around her thin waist and an itchy, blue visor that hides a small star tattoo on her right temple.

I name her Alice. She's nineteen and extremely dirty, a runaway since age fifteen. She places small asterisks on the ticket order when she wants to signal Lionel to meet her in the back room in eight minutes. The scent of cleaning supplies and dirty water wafts in the air as Lionel lifts her skirt and sticks his oily fingers inside her.

Her moans grow into something that mirrors the sound of a cat whose paw has gotten stuck inside a screen door: a piercing screech that causes Lionel to place his hand firmly against her mouth. Though young, Alice is extremely talented at taking all of Lionel in, squeezing her vaginal muscles like a tight fist, hiding a secret letter that no one but she can read. He feels completely swallowed as the tightness of her pussy fluctuates around him. She orgasms three times before he even has the chance to come inside her. She begs for his come because it makes her feel full and complete.

Alice is the type of girl who pleads for more, even when sore and dry. She flirts with customers and often encourages them to join her and Lionel in a little bit of fun. She prefers women, and after several weeks of fucking in the back room, or outside behind the Dumpster, Alice introduces a rotating array of breasts and pussies into the mix.

Lionel loves Alice and often thinks about her when masturbating at home. The other women are good, and watching her fuck them turns him on, but no one compares to her.

I imagine that for his birthday, she presents him with a key and a note. The instructions lead him to room eighteen at the Motel 8, where Alice waits with a regular customer from the restaurant named Jeanie. Jeanie is thirty-three, with two kids and occasional child support checks. This is her first time getting eaten out by a girl, but not her first time being watched during sex.

As the door opens, Lionel is greeted by a view of Alice's perfectly round and creamy ass rising into the air. A thick set of thighs squirms beneath her and Lionel listens to the sounds of Alice licking and eating away at another woman's cunt. There's no pause or interruption of any kind as Lionel enters the room, throws his jacket and keys on a chair, and removes all of his clothes.

He's hard and ready, and he jerks off to the vision of Alice and this woman entwined like flesh-covered pretzels. Alice flips around and Jeanie dives between her thighs, sticking her tongue and fingers into Alice's sopping cunt. Lionel doesn't know this, but it's at this moment that Jeanie decides she loves the taste of pussy. She loves it so much, in fact, that she is going to become obsessed with it. Jeanie will spend the next few months fucking as many women as possible, savoring the alternating flavors of women she has picked up at gay bars, grocery stores, and once, a bank.

Jeanie will become a cunt connoisseur, sharpening her palette for pussy. She'll know exactly what each woman eats each day just from her flavor. She will become infamous within the lesbian community and she'll eventually fall in love with a bulldyke named Chrys, who will completely change her vegan diet just for Jeanie, so that her come tastes better.

But no one knows this yet, especially Jeanie. At this very moment in room eighteen, all Lionel, Alice and Jeanie know is this: the scent of sweat and come wafting through the air, Lionel on all fours jerking himself off to the moans of Alice and Jeanie eating each other out simultaneously.

This is Lionel's best birthday ever.

After the time in the motel room, Alice and Lionel continue to fuck in as many places and positions as possible. Sometimes at the restaurant all they have time for is a quick blowjob. If it's slow and Lionel has backup in the kitchen, he'll force her down on all fours, sliding beneath her as if she's a Buick in need of an oil change. He'll slurp and lick and nibble on her clit until it grows in size. Her slippery lips will flap against his open mouth as she curves her hand behind her and sticks three to four fingers into his anus, his new favorite way to come. This preference formed after the time Alice fucked Lionel from behind using a strap-on named Harvey. It was red-and-black striped, and wide enough to cause Lionel to add a limp and swagger to his step for almost two weeks.

Or maybe Alice doesn't exist. Maybe there's no waitress who teaches Lionel the pleasures of anal sex. Maybe there's no motel room. No Jeanie. Maybe there are no women at all. Maybe Alice is really Jeremy, a new waiter working part-time to help pay for school. I imagine Jeremy to be in his first year of community college, eighteen, and extremely lanky. His voice sounds unformed and he has oily and spotted skin. Lionel isn't drawn to Jeremy because of looks or personality. The attraction is simply based upon the impressive bulge bending into Jeremy's zipper, and Lionel wants more of what he can't see.

In the third month of Jeremy's employment, Lionel stays later than usual and insists on helping the wait staff close up. He times his entrance into the back room just perfectly, walking in as Jeremy is wringing out the mop and pouring dirty water down the drain.

The scene will go something like this:

Lionel walks up behind Jeremy, pants already unzipped—cock pulled out and standing at attention after a few tugs—musing on the wonder and mystery of the possibility of Jeremy's over-sized dick pushing and rubbing against his black pants. Jeremy feels Lionel before he actually sees him. He doesn't turn around. There may have been a slight gasp or an inaudible mumble that isn't acknowledged.

"We're the only ones in here and that may not be for very long. Go behind the bulk sugar and flour shelves and take off your pants," Lionel instructs him.

Jeremy doesn't attempt a refusal. His long legs take just a few small steps before reaching the desired spot. He unbuckles his brown leather belt, pants falling to the floor, takes off his blue-checkered boxers and stands there in front of Lionel's hard-on, wearing only a shirt, socks and black converse sneakers. Lionel's thick cock climbs its way into him.

In the back room, Lionel fucks him in a way that makes Jeremy forget all about his girlfriend who never made him feel quite this good.

Jeremy turns around, feeling the warmth of Lionel's precome dripping down his thighs. He stares at the length and width of what was just inside him. He wants to taste it. He wants to know what he tastes like on Lionel.

Down on his knees, Jeremy takes Lionel's dick in his mouth, hands gripping his balls. He alternates licking and sucking and rubbing. Jeremy almost gags as Lionel thrusts his cock farther into Jeremy's mouth, enjoying the heat and rough surface of Jeremy's tongue around him. Lionel squeezes his thighs into Jeremy's neck just as he's about to come. The semen travels into Jeremy's mouth, down his throat, and it fertilizes Jeremy's insides. It tastes like sour milk and sea salt and sweat.

I'm in my bathroom sitting on the toilet, and the tiles are cold against my bare feet. I rest them beside the bathtub, which provides a perfect angle for my fingers to rise inside me. The lights are off and I see the tiny room only by the soft flicker of light from the small, unscented candles. The music? The soundtrack for this moment? It's Lionel Enthusiast III grunting like a sweaty boar covered in mud or come, depending upon circ*come*stance.

I've closed the bathroom door. I live alone, so there's no fear of being interrupted, but I want to feel contained. I want to feel as though the small square of this room is a body embracing me as I hold myself.

My accessories are inside the dry bathtub: purple vibrator with a three-speed setting and four dildos, all varying in size, width, and curvature. I hop off the toilet and slowly step into the porcelain tub. Its cold skin shocks my own and I shiver. I decide that my clit is cold, so I pick up dildo number two, seven inches of steel, lime green, and prewarmed. It's the one that always makes me come in record time.

I tease my clit by rubbing the dildo against it—softly at first, then pressing harder. I pretend my clitoris is a dick that expands when hard. It wants a blowjob. A hand job. It wants to penetrate as many holes as it can. It wants to get a girl pregnant. It wants to shoot a giant wad of come inside someone's mouth, cunt and anus.

I'm warm now and Lionel Enthusiast III is just on the other side of this wall. I touch the divider between us, press my face against the tile, pretending it's him. His skin. His cock. His belly. His chest. I moan.

The rhythmic grunting suddenly ceases. Has he heard me? I moan louder. He responds, or so it seems, with an ecstatic growl.

Maybe he hears me and thinks of Alice. Or maybe I want him to be Alice: nineteen-year-old flesh, crisp nipples that rise when licked or pinched. I pull on her hair so hard that several strands come off in my fingers. Alice tastes like a ripe Bartlett pear. She's bruised, but oozing flavor.

I imagine Jeanie walking in. I pretend to be surprised or flustered by her spontaneous entrance. She's like an Olympic swimmer, gracefully diving between my legs. Her three-inch tongue penetrates my cunt, her mouth mumbling the names of all the foods I've eaten today.

Sharp pecorino cheese. Spoonful of smooth peanut butter. No, wait—extra chunky. Two mugs of Earl Grey tea with cream and one teaspoon of sugar. Handful of chocolate chips. Half an avocado. Then, the other half with a sliced tomato that wasn't quite ripe yet. A banana.

Lionel is ravishing himself, watching Jeanie and me. His hand travels up and down his cock, palm like a trained pole dancer. His fingers stroke his balls as though they were made from loose tassels. I can hear the echo of his moans bounce against the wall.

Jeremy appears. He pushes my back up against the bathroom wall, skinny legs pressed against my thick ones. He grabs my neck and thrusts his hard cock inside me. I'm surprised at my ability to take him in. He sucks on my neck, making my clit jealous. He eventually works his way down.

The soundtrack ends. Lionel must have finished himself off. I have yet to orgasm, and I realize that it's the mystery of Lionel's actions that allow me to come with an explosive eruption. I want to bang on the wall and scream, "More! Keep going! Don't stop! I need this!"

I'm still in the bathtub, skin electrified by almost an hour of experimental fucking. Glass dildo replaces steel one. Then, the vibrator—almost numbing my clit as it throbs toward a quick orgasm. I need more. I want to gush all over the tub, fill it with my juices, my flavors. I want Lionel Enthusiast III and Alice and Jeanie and Jeremy to bust through my door and fuck me so hard that my spine breaks. I want to feel them inside me for days, weeks. I want to scream three coats of paint off my walls just from the force. I want them to need scuba gear as I drown them in the thick fluids rushing out from my cunt.

I'm never meant to meet Lionel Enthusiast III. I never find out what he looks like, or what he really does as his profession. I never learn how close I am to guessing his sexual preference for position or person. I never knock on our shared wall and ask him to finish me off.

In four months, I move into a one-bedroom apartment with a woman who I meet at the grocery store. Her name is Joanna and she's much taller than I. Our first conversation is about kumquats, which I confess I originally thought was a sexual position. She laughs and I notice the small dimple on her right cheek. She tells me its origin is a Chinese evergreen shrub and I only half listen, becoming fixated on her dimple and the thickness of her fingers and how incredible they would feel inside me. I wonder how strong she is and if she could lift me high enough so that my cunt would line right up against her mouth and does she even fancy the flavor of ripe pussy and—

Our first date ends with her tongue drifting from inside my mouth to inside my cunt to beneath my armpit to below my neck. I feel the warm power of her fingers pressing into me. One, then two, then three, moving in and out until I beg for her to finish me off. Make me come. I cover her bare flesh with everything that has been brewing inside me, everything that Lionel has inspired.

Joanna sucks on her fingers and places them inside her pussy, as I drive my face into her bush. It smells like a rain forest, a mix of fiddlehead ferns and wood shavings. We fall asleep with the scent of each other on our faces and bodies.

After a month, she says *I love you* for the first time. In three, we move in together. I forget about the wall—my bathroom adventures, the soundtrack of Lionel and his low-octave pleasure moans. Everything becomes lost, until the day Joanna tells me a story about my next-door neighbor.

WHERE THE RUBBER MEETS THE ROAD

Aimee Pearl

We're walking down the street and he's fucking me. Everything's slippery and delicious.

This is all true.

We're at the Folsom Street Fair—the annual outdoor kink-fest—and it's a hot San Francisco September day, hot in a way that only San Francisco can be, and only in September, a wet heat. There's a swelling between my legs. He's going to make me gush.

We're walking in broad daylight. The crowd is thick around us. He rubs a wet thumb against my clit. We move side by side in stride, no pauses. I wonder...

If anyone looked down toward my crotch, they might see his right hand sneaking around the edge of my bright cherry red latex micromini. They might realize that he's got a finger sliding between my lower lips. What would they think? What would they say?

My skirt is so short that it doesn't cover the full curve of my ass. You can see my cheeks peeking out from the bottom of the shiny rubber coating. I can't wear panties in this, and I can't sit. Can only stand. Can only keep on walking. While he fucks me.

He's devilishly handsome, this one. His skin is the color of a toasted hazelnut, and twice as tasty. We've fucked many times before, but never like this. Never outdoors, in the middle of the street, digits stretching wet rubber wide.

The red of my skirt is polished to a gleam, and I love the way the color looks metallic against my velvet-soft brown skin. This was the first piece of latex I ever bought, the first one I ever tried on. Its tightness around my narrow waist, rounded hips, and plump ass makes me look and feel space-alien-exotic, and draws attention to the fullest part of my body. Yes, my butt has stopped traffic. Who doesn't like to look at a black diva in red rubber?

For now, though, we're blending in, seeping into the throng around us. He's giving me a teasing fuck and my cunt is starting to ache with desire. Pretty soon, I'll want more fingers, I'll want to swallow his fist whole. We've got to find a doorway to lean into. I can't come while walking. I'm perched on spiked heels and might fall over.

The orgasms he gives me have been known to cause great commotion.

We find an alley and he pounds me quick and hard, leaves me wet and feeling dirty. This boy has a way with those hands of his. He once made me come while I prepared a cup of tea, holding the kettle, boiling hot and full, precariously. He came behind me at the stove and rammed four fingers into me. Undid me. Unraveled me. I don't know how I managed to pour steady after that.

But I did.

We're discovered in our crevice by onlookers, dykes from

around town, smiling at the queer couple that is us. I wish he was packing, so that we could give 'em a real show. Unfortunately, he left his dick at home today. Who needs it, I guess, when you've got hands like his?

Still, I do crave his cock sometimes. For a moment, as he fucks me roughly one more time for our audience, I imagine him, silicone in hand, rubbing his rubber-covered rubber dick against my rubber-covered rear. Rolling up latex for greater access. Sliding toy into tightness. A fetishistic ass-fuck on a city street, sweaty.

I do it again. Come.

Later, we leave our alley love nest and slide back into the crowded thoroughfare. He runs into a friend, a gorgeous high femme white girl with a buzz cut. Six two in heels, she works as a pro-domme at a local dungeon. Today is her day off, and she and her girlfriend/submissive are strolling through the fair. She's wearing an ankle-length latex dress, and she's drenched in sweat. She squats down and lifts her skirt to circulate air around her sweet blonde pussy. I want to swoon, but not from the heat. She complains about the weather, and about the clients who keep spotting her in the crowd and begging to be dominated.

Beside me, he chats casually with her and smiles. He knows I'm a sucker for a pissed-off femme domme, not to mention one wearing more even latex than I am. From my angle above her, I can see down into her cleavage and admire the beads of wetness on her full breasts. I'm starting to feel wet again myself. He knows. He knows it's time to fuck me again. He knows it's time to go for a walk.

On our next date, we meet at midnight, this time in another alley, in a different part of town. He's hanging out in a club up the street; I've been instructed to drive into the alley and wait for him in the backseat. I send him a text to let him know I've arrived, and arrange myself to be ready for him. He leaves the club and approaches my car.

I'm wearing a cream-colored knee-length A-line leather skirt. The material is so soft and buttery that most admirers don't even recognize that it's made out of leather—at first glance anyway. This skirt always gets a second glance. It's not short, it's not tight, and it's not an eye-catching color. But it manages to exude a subtle sexiness. It's a great skirt for a dominant woman to wear, because of its strict lines. But I'm a submissive, and I like to wear it to feel encased in it, bound by the leather, however loosely, as it falls around my thighs.

There's a rap at the window, and I reach over to unlock the door and let him in. Let him get in. Let him come in and fuck me.

As requested, I'm not wearing any panties, although this time it's not because of the length of my skirt, of course, but because of other constraints of the scene. Namely, he wants quick and easy access to my cunt; he wants to fuck me quickly and then leave me to go back to his friends at the club. It's all been prearranged. We move like we're dancing. Only there's no music, just the sound of leather rubbing against vinyl, and breathing. His breath and mine—mostly mine as he's fucking me hard and I'm struggling to endure it, to take it all in. He's packing this time, all right, using one of his biggest cocks.

The day was hot but the night is cold. The windows steam over, and, as I'm parked illegally in a one-way dimly lit alley, I'm beginning to worry if we'll attract any unwanted attention. He doesn't seem to be concerned. He was cavalier from the moment he entered the car. He hasn't said a word to me, in fact. Just leapt in, closed and locked the door behind him, shoved me down onto my stomach, and used one hand to pull his cock out while the other pushed my skirt up.

He's gripping my skirt, the thin leather bunched into his fist. One of my arms is pinned under me, but with my other I start to reach out and run my hand along his pant leg. I discover he's wearing leather chaps over his jeans, and that they fit nice and snug. I try to reach far enough to get to the edge of the leather, so I can stroke his crotch. But he's not having any of this, doesn't want me to move. He rams his cock into me to the hilt and uses both his arms to hold me down, immobilizing me. My face is buried in the vinyl of the seat, my legs spread wide with one on the seat and the other leaning over the side toward the floor, and all else is sound and heat and motion and fullness. His chaps are rubbing the vinyl, my skirt is rubbing the vinyl, and there's no room to breathe. I'm gasping for air, wondering which one of us will come first, when suddenly, without warning, he pulls out.

He pulls out, and pulls back, and I can finally catch my breath. But I'm confused. I shift around to see what's going on, and witness him pulling two things out of his pockets. My eyes go wide as I see that one is a rubber ball gag, and the other is a small packet of my favorite anal-sex lube. He lays the lube packet on my bare ass and speaks for the first time all night.

"Open up."

I open my mouth to receive the gag, and then he secures the straps in place at the back of my head. Now he twists the tab off the lubricant and dribbles it onto his dick. His second sentence comes at me:

"Get ready."

The head of his cock is already pressing against my asshole. When we talked about meeting in the alley, he said he wanted things to go quickly. But if he's seriously thinking of fucking my ass with that big toy, this is going to take a while.

Or so I think.

He works it in with surprising speed. Behind the gag, I'm

grunting and half screaming, but he knows I can take it, and I know he's going to make me. The perverse thrill of submitting to this sadistic "forced" ass-fuck actually causes me to open a little more, which eases his way inside. He's one step ahead of me, and pushes as I acquiesce.

When his cock is completely in my ass, he pauses for a moment, to give me a chance to feel the extent to which he's stretched me out, to confirm my own surrender. One moment, and then it's over. That's all I get. After that, it's his turn.

He pounds me hard, fucking me for all he's worth. He's determined to come and he knows how to use my ass for his own pleasure. My job is to endure. Gagged, held down, plowed, I am a thing to him. An object. A leather-clad fuck-hole. He slams into my ass, over and over, until he shoots his orgasm into me. It's not liquid, of course; it's an energy, and thus, twice as potent. I take every drop, deep into my ass, for him.

And when he's done, he pulls out gently, undoes my gag gently, slides me over onto my back gently, smoothes down my skirt gently, and gently, very gently, reaches under my skirt and flicks one slick finger against my clit.

I explode.

I come against his hand with a roar, violent waves of pleasure crashing onto me. He holds me as I come, body to body, gripping me tightly until my moans subside.

Then, just as quickly as he entered, he puts his dick back in his pants, zips up, and leaves.

ON MY KNEES IN BARCELONA

Kristina Lloyd

This happened before the '92 Summer Olympics in Barcelona, when the nights were so hot the city couldn't sleep and everyone grew angry and crazy. Zero tolerance was just a rumor, so whores, thieves and smackheads skulked in narrow streets and everyone avoided the docks. I only went to Bar Anise in the hope they'd give me some ice. Had I known what kind of bar it was, I might have stayed away.

It was nearly 2:00 a.m. and I was standing on my dinky balcony, feeling pretty zonked. The fuse had gone in my fan and the air in my apartment felt thick enough to slice. In the street below, a globe lamp hung like a moon on a bracket, adding a sheen of pearl to the facade of Bar Anise. I held a damp cloth to the back of my neck, arms resting on metal too hot to touch during the day. Earlier, the cloth had contained fast-melting ice and my mind returned to the cold rivulets trickling over my shoulders, collarbone and breasts. Like a tongue, I'd thought, the tongue of a lover making whoopee with my skin. How long had it been now? Oh, too many months to count.

Six floors below, footsteps echoed in the dark street. I watched a guy in a white T-shirt stride along with a sense of purpose unsuited to the hour. When he suddenly looked up I was unnerved, feeling a rupture of that odd balance where my balcony is at once part of the street and part of my home. It was as if he'd barged in on my privacy.

I turned away, embarrassed to have been caught watching, then glanced back to see him enter Bar Anise. A relic from another age, the bar's exterior glowed with low-watt tones of honey and oak, its door closed, its windows pasted with faded posters, that globe lamp fuzzed with a halo of white light. As the guy pushed the door, I half expected the structure to wobble like a stage set.

How come I'd never been in before? Generally speaking, I socialized in Barcelona's hipper bars along Las Ramblas, in Plaça Reial or Barri Gòtic, and I only ventured into local bars to buy late-night beers or water. They were down-at-heel joints with Formica tabletops, fruit machines and a TV tuned permanently to the lotto draw. I fancied Bar Anise was different but I'd never set foot inside. Oh, sure, I was curious but the place seemed to exist in a world of its own. It may as well have had No ENTRY on its door.

At 2:00 a.m., however, it was the only bar open.

I wiped the damp cloth over my face, reminding myself I was lucky to be single and sleeping alone. Along my street, shabby ironwork balconies were cluttered with blushing geraniums, cramped little washing lines, green roller blinds and even a bird in a cage three buildings to my right. In these Spanish homes, behind the old lace at the windows, the occupants probably slept two to a bed, sticky bodies wrestling with hot, tangled sheets. Yes, in this heat, I was lucky to be single. Some ice to see me through the night would be welcome though. Unfortunately, my ice compartment was empty so I had to ask myself: how badly did I want it?

My sandals were noisy in the deserted street, ringing off walls and metal shutters. I hesitated before the door of Bar Anise, disconcerted by the sense of stillness beyond. A sign in Catalan proclaimed the bar open but was it really? And if so, was it open to the likes of me? In those months, I was working as a sub-editor on a weekly expat newspaper called *Gander*. Prior to that, I'd spent three years teaching English in Seville until I'd tired of both the work and a boyfriend who'd kept the fingernails long on his right hand so he could simultaneously learn Spanish guitar and repulse me. Sometimes, I felt at home in that foreign land but when I stood on the threshold of Bar Anise, I felt I'd just arrived from Mars.

I considered quitting, then recalled those tongues of molten ice trailing across my skin. Taking a deep breath, I entered. Cigarette smoke hung in the yellowing light and a ceiling fan turned sluggishly as if enervated by the heat. Half a dozen men sat alone at separate tables, smoking, reading or staring into space. No one paid me any notice and I was grateful. I took it to be one of those places where everyone is a stranger, even people who've been drinking side by side for years.

When I approached the counter with my empty jug, a customer seated there cast me a look of lazy appraisal. He wore a white T-shirt and I took him to be the guy I'd seen from my balcony. Big nosed with dark hair feathering across his forehead, his wrinkles added interest to a strong, angular face. But irrespective of rugged charm, middle-aged men who believe they're entitled to leer unsettle my confidence. I was self-conscious in asking for ice and when my request was met with a frown, I stumbled in repeating myself. The bartender wiped the counter with a cloth, apparently loath to serve me. Behind him, among shelves gleaming with bottles and glasses, a mirrored Coca-Cola clock said quarter past two. The clock's red logo gave me that old jolt of jarring familiarity, making me feel I was on territory at once homely and strange.

"I have money," I said.

With that, the bartender disappeared into an adjoining room, a curtain of plastic strips clattering lightly as he passed. I waited, wondering if the drinkers could see the ice tonguing my skin; if they could see me at night, water coursing over my flesh; if they could see how I tried to kill the heat of my longing, failing as the ice melted away and I climaxed once again.

I felt they could and it troubled me. On the counter, a wedge of tortilla sat forlornly under a plastic dome. I could hear the bartender on the phone in the adjoining room. All this for some ice? When he returned with my jug blissfully full, I asked how much I owed him. Before he could reply, Big Nose interrupted, addressing the bartender in Catalan, a language I wasn't yet familiar with. The bartender poured a large brandy, then set it in front of me.

"Gratis," he said.

Unwilling to risk offence, I accepted the drink while trying to convince myself it left me under no obligation. So bloody English of me. Why couldn't I decline the brandy, pay for the ice conventionally and leave?

"Graçias," I said, turning to the customer, but I didn't smile.

He nodded, lips tilting in wry amusement. The brandy was rough, its heat scorching my throat and blazing inside my chest. The nape of my neck was wet with sweat, my hair damp. I was concerned about the ice melting in my jug and wished I could sip the ice water. The ceiling fan clicked faintly. Nobody spoke and

I was relieved. It could simply be this guy was silently extending the hand of friendship. If so, I would silently shake it then shoot off home. The brandy was difficult to drink though, fire when I wanted ice.

"*Ay, qué calor,*" said my new friend at length.

"*Sí, qué calor,*" I replied.

Hot weather. I sipped my brandy. I could feel him watching and his passive interest bugged me. After a couple more minutes, wanting to escape his gaze, I asked for the *lavabos* and was directed down a flight of rickety stairs. I descended toward a basement with scruffy, dark crimson walls, toilets at the far end and a swinging door with a small, dirty window lined with wire mesh. Halfway down the stairs, movement below caught my eye. I paused, looking over my shoulder at the corridor behind me. Beyond an open door was a guy on a chair and a woman on her knees, her head bobbing in his lap. I clutched the banister, immobilized by fear and a sudden, pornographic lust.

My cunt swelled and swelled, blood throbbing there. Oh, Christ, what a picture. The guy's mouth was slack, his head tipped back, as the woman, her chestnut curls fanning over his thighs, dipped up and down, up and down. Had they heard me? Hell, I hoped not. I needed to watch. Until that moment, I hadn't known how much I wanted cock; hadn't known how much I'd missed it since dumping the guitarist; hadn't known that stab of raging desire. Because while I could fuck myself with cock-shaped objects (cool as a cucumber), nothing could ever come close to the overwhelming sensations of a deep, dark, blinding mouthful. I stared, hardly daring to breathe.

The guy was young and lean, a tumble of ink black curls giving him an air of flamenco passion. Transfixed, I watch him grow fiercer, pulling the woman onto him, his fingers snarled in her hair as his pelvis rocked either to meet or defeat her. In her kneeling position, the woman kicked at the floor, squealing in muffled protest, her hands flapping. My yearning for cock was knocked for six by a second wave, a shocking urge to be claimed and used in a myriad of filthy ways.

My cunt flared to a cushiony mass of need, so sensitive I fancied I could feel the warp and weft of cotton in my underwear. I wanted to be where she was, at the mercy of a wild stranger who regarded me as nothing but an object for his pleasure, insignificant and disposable. I wanted to be all body and no mind, a thing made of cunt, mouth and ass, wide open and ready to receive.

Face aflame, I turned, intending to hurry back to the bar. I would put it from my thoughts, pretend nothing had happened, pretend I hadn't seen either the couple or the grubby depths of my desire. Was this because I hadn't had sex for so long? Was I craving the basest sort of action as compensation for those months of lack? Feeling shaky, I clasped the banister, mouth dry as a bone.

My stomach somersaulted. To my horror, at the head of the stairs stood the big-nosed guy from the bar. He grinned, descending in slow, swaggering steps. Panicking, I glanced down to the room. The guy in the chair was looking right at me, smirking as he slammed the woman's head between his thighs. My knees turned wobbly while blood pumped in my ears, roaring like seashells and high fever.

Big Nose was at my side, his forehead gleaming with a film of sweat. He tipped his eyebrows at me. *"Cuatro miles pesetas,"* he said.

Outrage spiked my fear. Four thousand pesetas! He thought I was a whore, thought I would blow him for a nasty brandy and a handful of notes!

"Déjame paso!" I snapped, attempting to sidestep him.

He mirrored me, blocking my path. I grew more afraid then, trapped between these two randy *cucarachas,* and yet my groin was pulsing as hard as my heart.

"*Cuatro miles,*" he repeated, nodding toward the basement room. Then in Spanish he added, "Take it, go on. It is a good price. You know you want it."

And I understood at once that I was to pay; that I was the punter not the whore. I didn't know whether to be more or less insulted. I stared at him, incredulous. He actually thought I was so desperate for cock I would pay to suck off a stranger in a sleazy, backstreet bar!

"Move," I said, no longer bothering to speak his language. Despite being on a lower step, I tried shouldering him out of the way but with swift skill, he jostled me backward. I cried out to realize I was now sandwiched between him and the wall, his chest pressing against my breasts, my arms trapped in his hands. For several seconds we stood there, our breaths shallow and tense.

"*No me molestes,*" I said, a Berlitz phrase I'd never had to use before.

The guy laughed and with good reason. My demand sounded so pitifully insincere I may as well have said, "Molest me." He crooked a finger, resting it in the hollow of my throat, and I turned aside, looking past him to the room below. The woman was watching us. She wiped the back of her hand across her mouth and laughed, white teeth flashing. I was relieved to see she wasn't in trouble but, more than that, I was relieved to see I wasn't the only woman keen on skirting so close to danger.

I turned to face Big Nose with renewed bravery but he trailed his bent finger up my neck. My skin tingled to his touch, tiny shivers of pleasure rippling through my body's heat. I tried defying him, tried steeling myself against his advances, but I caught the sadistic brightness in his bitter chocolate eyes and I melted a little more. I pressed my head back to the wall.

"*No me molestes,*" I repeated, my voice soft and tremulous.

He laughed quietly, his breath tickling my face. I wanted him to touch me in horrible ways, to stick his hand between my thighs or paw my breasts. But he didn't. He just reiterated his price. When I didn't reply, he ground his crotch against me, rubbing his hard-on above the swell of my pubis. The pressure of him there distilled to my cunt, making my lips part and pout.

"*Qué barato!*" he said. A good price.

The basement was hot as hell. Sweat prickled on my back, cotton clinging damply. He knew he was turning me on and every rock of his body was sweet torture, twisting me with what I didn't want to want.

In Spanish, I said, "I just came for ice. I need to go home now. Release me, please."

"You will not sleep," he replied. "It's too hot."

"I have ice."

"You don't want ice," he said. "You want cock."

I felt the color rise in my face. He placed his hands either side of my head, caging me loosely in his arms, his biceps forming swarthy little hillocks on the edges of my vision. A waft of sweat, earthy and masculine, surged into my senses and I wanted to bury my nose in his armpits and inhale him.

"There's cock here," he continued. "Take it, *guapa*. We are not expensive. Take what you want then go home."

His eyes were such a deep brown I could barely distinguish pupil from iris.

"I don't have much money on me," I said.

He chuckled and I flushed deeper to realize I'd betrayed myself.

"Then go get some money," he said. "There's a cash machine—"

"No," I murmured.

"Yes, stop resisting yourself. Do you agree it is a fair price?"

"I don't know," I whispered, and I genuinely didn't. It seemed an amount I'd pay without too many qualms. But fair, good? There was no market value for this; it flew in the face of the usual sexism dictating the flow of supply and demand: women give, men get. Without a scarcity of clean men with hard cocks, why would I pay? And what in the world would prompt a cock-drought? Guys were always up for it. But here and now in the early hours in Bar Anise, they'd changed the world, creating both a need and a scarcity. Demand outstripped supply. A fair price? The thud in my pussy insisted it was a bargain.

I swallowed. "I have money in my *piso,*" I said, deeply ashamed. "I live across the street."

He stepped back. "Vete!" he said, gesturing up the stairs.

I wasted no time, striding through the bar, head held high. At that point, I was unsure if I would return. I thought I might come to my senses but the night was sultry and weighted with the city, its heat wrapping me in strange enchantments where Bar Anise's subterranean secrets seduced me away from the prosaic. The man's voice echoed in my mind: Stop resisting yourself.

Gone was the Barcelona I knew where the metro whisked me to work, sunshine poured on mosaic lizards, plane trees shimmered and cathedral spires and scaffolding stabbed a flat blue sky. Instead, lust conspired with magic and menace to lead me as if in a dream to collect money from my apartment and scurry back to the bar.

Stop resisting yourself.

I downed the brandy still awaiting me on the counter and crept downstairs, my sordid hunger flaring at the wine-dark walls and scents of sweat and semen lingering in the shadows.

All I'm doing, I told myself, is buying sex much as men have done for centuries. Nonetheless, I felt myself less an empowered consumer and more a desperate, greedy slut, a woman shameless enough to slake her desire in this masculine habitat of beer, cigarettes and sullen, perceptible misogyny. But I liked that these guys probably didn't much care for me except as an object to fuck. The feeling was mutual.

No one was about in the basement so, nervously, I entered the room I'd seen earlier, an underused storeroom with drums of olive oil lined against a wall, boxes under a large wooden table and four towers of orange chairs stacked in a corner. Big Nose was sitting spread-legged on a reversed chair, arms folded on its back. Behind him on the table sat his flamenco-looking friend, one leg swinging back and forth. My heart was going nineteen to the dozen.

"Who takes the money?" I asked.

Big Nose held out a hand. Feigning confidence, I gave him the notes. Stretching, he passed them to Flamenco who bundled them into his jeans pocket as if he were the pimp. There was a brief exchange in Catalan and I understand only that it was about money and that Big Nose was called Jordi.

"*Graçias,*" said Flamenco, relaxing his posture to suggest his work was done.

Jordi stood and spun the chair to face me. Still standing, he said, "On your knees."

I glanced at Flamenco who was making no moves to leave. "It's not a floor show," I said.

Jordi grabbed my face with a broad hand, forcing me to meet his gaze. He squeezed my cheeks. "On your fucking knees."

His nastiness sent shards of arousal to my groin. I felt bullied and debased, even more so because of our audience, and it was everything I wanted but would never have dared ask for. I fell to my knees, the scuffed hardwood floor briefly cooling my skin. Ahead of me, the fly of Jordi's jeans undulated over his boner, the faded denim at his crotch reminding me how much of a stranger he was, the rhythms of a life unknown imprinted on fabric concealing the cock I was about to blow. With a clink of metal, he unbuckled and unzipped, rummaging to release his erection.

My heart gave a kick of joy at the sight of his hard-on raging up from the wiry thicket of his pubes. I'd forgotten how obscenely aggressive hard cocks are and his was a brutish beauty, the color suffusing the head with such intensity I fancied it might seep through his skin to stain the air with a blood violet hue. He gripped himself, fingers thick around his girth, the sea blue vein on his underside peeping as he gently jerked.

"It's a good price, no?" he said.

Doing my best to forget about Flamenco, I opened my mouth to take Jordi but he stilled me with a hand on my forehead. "It's a good price," he repeated sternly.

His balls were tucked up tight and they lifted as he worked his shaft.

"*Sí, sí, claro,*" I replied.

He clasped my head and drew me sharply onto his cock. The sudden fullness of my mouth made me splutter and he held me there, forcing me to inhale his humidity and that smell I'd forgotten, the smell of men, a smell reminiscent of depths and of things discarded, of dark oceans, forest floors, dereliction, old tires and knives left out in the sun.

"*Así me gusta, nena,*" he said approvingly as I withdrew to his tip.

He held my head, adding a slight pressure as I began slurping back and forth, making it seem as if he were the one leading. Perhaps he was. That seemed at odds with me being the paying customer but I enjoyed him taking the upper hand, so perhaps the incongruity was superficial.

"Qué bonita," said Flamenco. How pretty.

Those watching eyes inflamed a shame that fueled my lust. I swallowed Jordi as deep as I could, my appetite provoking him to greater force. He began fucking my face, driving into my instinctive resistance, making me whimper and cough as my saliva spilled and my eyes watered. I felt sluttish and used, at the mercy of these callous brutes, and it was bliss. My swollen cunt was so fat and rich it barely seemed to have room between my thighs.

"Hey, Àngel," said Jordi, addressing his friend. "Why don't you give her a free fuck? You would like this, *nena? Es gratis!"*

He withdrew from my mouth to let me speak.

"Sí, sí, fóllame!" I croaked, gazing up at Jordi through a veil of tears. He sat heavily in the chair, lowering my head to his height. I dropped onto all fours, engulfing his length again while hoping the free fuck would be as hot and rough as the free brandy.

I heard Àngel cross the room. Àngel. What a perfect, preternatural name for this other-worldly scenario. Taking position behind me, Àngel flipped up my skirt and yanked down my underwear. I groaned around Jordi's cock and his answering groan echoed in my ears. I heard Àngel unzip and I shuffled my knees wider, groaning again when he teased me by slotting his cock to the length of my folds. He sawed to and fro, the upward strain of his erection pressing into my wetness and making me ache for penetration.

Àngel spoke to Jordi in Catalan, tight hard words muttered under his breath. Jordi replied, throaty and urgent. With a sound like an expletive, Àngel slammed into me, hissing as he lodged himself high. He was meaty and solid and he clasped my hips, gripping hard as he began driving into my hole. Every thrust jolted my body, jerking me forward onto Jordi's lap. I felt skewered all the way through, my mouth and cunt both stuffed to capacity. The two men worked together, fucking, pushing, grunting and groaning. Occasionally they exchanged words I didn't understand and once or twice there was amusement and faint laughter.

They had me. They well and truly had me. And when Àngel reached for my clit, I knew I was lost. My climax raced closer and I bleated with nearness. Àngel hissed in Catalan. Jordi growled.

"*Sigue, sigue,*" he said. He grabbed fistfuls of my hair, his cock swelling to its absolute limit in my mouth. I was a rag doll between the two men, so close to coming my limbs seemed to have lost their bones. With a hoarse cry, Jordi came, flooding my mouth with his bitter silk, and the sound of his release tipped me over the edge. I came hard, disoriented and dizzy as pleasure clutched and stars exploded in my mind.

Moments later, my body began to drop with exhaustion but there was no letup from Àngel. He kept fucking me like there was no tomorrow and my pulpy walls, swollen with sensitivity, clung to his thrusts. I held Jordi in my mouth, gasping on his dwindling erection until Àngel's hammering became so frenzied I fancied he wanted to destroy me. He peaked with a long, low groan, wedging himself deep, and I moaned around Jordi's cock, wishing I could melt clean away.

The three of us held still until Jordi stroked my hair, a tender gesture that took me by surprise. Àngel caressed my buttocks. For a minute or two, we rested in silence and in those moments, I felt we shared a tacit understanding and mutual respect. We had all got what we wanted and were grateful.

But I didn't want to stay. I had nothing to say to them, nor them to me. Conversation would have made us awkward and I wanted to leave it there, pure and perfect, a moment out of time devoted entirely to pleasure. Àngel slipped away and I tidied myself up. Jordi asked how I was. I told him I was fine just as Àngel returned with my jug, full to the brim with ice. There was no one in the bar when I left and all the lights were off. Jordi unlocked the door so I could leave.

"*Graçias,*" I said.

"*De nada,*" he replied with a smile. "*Y graçias.*"

Back in my apartment, I tipped half the ice into a freezer bag, stashed it in my ice compartment, and took the remaining ice to bed. I thought I would do my usual routine of rubbing cubes over my skin to cool me into sleep but I must have crashed out at once. In the morning, my jug contained only water and my mind was a fog of lust and filth. Where had I been? What had I done? Did that actually happen?

I slipped on a T-shirt, rolled up my shutter and stepped out onto my balcony. It was early morning but already the heat pulsed like the midday sun. I rubbed my eyes. Below, the street was coming to life, the baker's window lined with breads and pastries, people heading to work, a woman on a Vespa turning left. I could see a couple of bars were open but not Bar Anise. It looked as if it hadn't been open for years, its facade concealed by chipboard, graffiti and tatty fly posters. Of course. Hadn't it always been derelict, just another dump waiting to be spruced up before the Olympics?

Drowsily, I padded to the kitchen. Had it been a dream then, just a crazy dream brought on by the heat? I withdrew the bag of ice from my fridge and went back to bed. I had another hour before work. I broke the ice into the jug, scooped up a handful and cupped it to my skin. Just a dream, I told myself, and I lay back on the pillows, wondering if the heat would transport me to Bar Anise on nights to come.

I smeared the ice over my skin, savoring the trickle of water melting onto my stomach. I murmured softly, imagining the touch was the lick of a lover. Just a dream. Words floated to me as if from a great distance. Stop resisting yourself. And I slid an ice cube up my neck then sucked it into my mouth, closing my eyes as I twirled my tongue around the cube, ice when I wanted fire.

MAN ABOUT TOWN

Amie M. Evans

"Come here," Joe said, leaning against the doorway to his bedroom, hard hat still in hand from his drag performance at Club Kit Kat's competition.

Tina, standing five feet away with her back toward him, seductively undid the zipper of her slinky dress and allowed it to slide down her body to pool on the floor.

"No," Tina said, faking a pout as she turned around revealing her red lace bra and lack of panties, before bursting into giggles.

Joe closed the gap between them with two long steps. Grabbing Tina, he tumbled both of them onto the bed. "Tell me no, will you," he said, climbing on top of her and pinning her wrists while the hard dildo under his jeans pushed against her leg.

They kissed. Joe continued, licking his way down her neck until he reached her cleavage. Tina's full, curvaceous body squirmed under him. He released her wrists to fondle double-D breasts then pushed the lace cups off of them, exposing tiny pink nipples. Tina's hands on the back of Joe's head pulled him closer. Joe sucked on a nipple, worked it with his tongue, and lightly nibbled on it. Tina squirmed under him, grinding her hips into his. He released her nipple and slid down her until dropping to his knees on the floor. Joe pushed her legs apart.

"What's the nasty construction worker going to do to me?" Tina asked. She loved the fantasy of having sex in character, and that Joe was always in drag when they went out.

"I won the contest, now I get my prize," Joe said before ripping Tina's panty hose open at the crotch, causing her to squeal in delight.

Tina's bush was the same red color as the long, flowing hair on her head. Carefully, Joe spread her full labia then stuck his tongue into her waiting hole. He probed gently, taking in her taste and scent. Licking up to her clit, Joe worked it in a tight circle with light, but firm strokes. He wanted to excite Tina but didn't want to make her come, at least, not yet. Slipping one finger into her cunt, Joe stroked in and out a few times. He added another finger and repeated the motion. Tina's moans became significantly louder. Joe stopped.

Standing up, he undid his jeans, allowing them to fall to his ankles, then pulled the dildo out of the opening of his blue boxer briefs. Tina positioned herself in the middle of the bed and Joe got on top. Using one hand, he inserted the peach-colored dildo into her wet cunt. Tina moaned as the head plunged into her. The shaft followed. Joe quickly stroked in and out, watching Tina's contorted facial expressions, listening to her quickened breathing, and loving that he was able to give her pleasure. After a few hard, long strokes, Joe pulled out.

He dropped to his knees again and yanked her ass to the edge of the bed. Tina placed her legs on his shoulders. Joe stuck three fingers into her cunt, also working her clit in hard, fast circles with his skilled tongue. Lacing her fingers into his short, brown hair, Tina shoved his face closer into her pelvis and groaned. Her hips began to rock quickly. She sucked in air and held it right before she came, thrusting her hips forward. Joe was careful not to get his nose broken by her vehemence, and not to stop stroking Tina's clit until he had coaxed a full, sopping orgasm from her. He did, however, stop thrusting his fingers into her, keeping them inside still and motionless as wave after wave of strong vaginal contractions were felt when she came.

Joe slipped his fingers out and lay next to Tina, cuddling her in his arms. He could just make out the faint smell of vanilla with a hint of rose, her familiar trademark scent, over the smells of sex and sweat.

In a few minutes, she would get up, as usual, and get dressed. Perhaps they'd share a glass of wine and talk about the drag show, but just as likely not. Since they were at Joe's, Tina would leave. This was the rhythm of their fucking. Joe did Tina. Sometimes Joe let Tina suck his dildo, but more likely, he just did her.

Tina rolled over so she was half on top of Joe. Her hair hung down tickling his face. "My turn," she said. Joe assumed she wanted to suck his dildo, but Tina forcefully pulled at it attempting to remove it from his pants.

"What?" he asked, pushing her hand away.

"My turn," she repeated, stroking the side of his face. "Let me, please, it doesn't matter if you come. I want to taste your pussy."

"No way," Joe barked, jumping up and moving across the room as he tucked his dildo back in. "No fucking way," he yelled, as he jerked up his pants.

"Joe," Tina said as she stood up, arms akimbo. "Come on. Trust me." She took a deep breath then exhaled. "Sweetie, whatever it is, it will be all right."

"Forget it. I won't let you." Joe crossed his arms on his chest.

"Fine." Tina started to put on her dress. "I can't do this anymore."

She looked at him. He looked back at her. Neither moved nor spoke. After a long, tenuous moment, Tina zipped her dress and left the room. Joe followed her into the living room, his arms still crossed. Putting her coat on, Tina made no eye contact with Joe. He grabbed her purse from the sofa before she could.

"Give it to me," Tina demanded, one arm extended.

"Can't we at least talk about this?"

"What's to talk about? I thought you'd eventually let me, at least once, try."

Joe put the purse in her hand.

"Will you?"

"No." Joe looked down at the floor. "You don't understand, Tina."

"No, Joe, I do. I understand completely. I just can't do this." Tina walked to the door and paused with her hand on the knob. "You don't understand that I like pussy. I like to please my lover."

"You please me. You have no idea how much you please me."

Tina shook her head, opened the door, walked out, and closed it behind her. She was gone.

Joe stood there, not moving, looking at the door as if at any second it would open and she'd reappear. After a few minutes, he walked over, turned the lock then returned to his bedroom. He removed all of his clothing, harness and dildo, and unwrapped his chest binding. With the light still on, he crawled between the sheets.

Joe and Tina had been dating for almost four months. While they'd been having sex since the second week of their romance, they'd never spent the night together. Joe had to get up early for work and Tina, who worked at night, slept late. This wasn't the real reason for Joe's reluctance to sleep over though. It was just a good excuse, allowing him to avoid revealing the truth about himself and to continue to protect himself from being exposed to what he perceived as a vulnerable situation if Tina awoke before him. So Joe had begged off sleepovers from the start and, like much in their relationship, not sleeping over had become a pattern. Just like Joe fucking Tina and not getting fucked himself, only seeing each other once a week on the night of the drag show, and Tina not meeting any of his old friends from before his drag king days, had all become patterns. And these patterns weren't mentioned or questioned, until, that is, this night.

Joe lay on his bed staring at the ceiling. Normally, after Tina and he had sex, once he'd gotten home or she'd left, Joe would get rid of his boxer briefs, take off his harness and dildo, remove his tight panty to release his own flesh-and-blood cock, and lay on his bed in the dark. Taking his cock in his lubed right hand, he would replay his sexual encounter with Tina in his head and masturbate himself to a proper orgasm. This night, however, the fight with Tina was the only thing he replayed.

Joe didn't know what to do. He could break up with Tina and find a new girlfriend. A number of the women who attended the drag shows had regularly offered to go home with him. But Joe feared he'd just be reliving the same fight with one of them in a few months. He'd also thought he was falling in love with Tina.

She was different from every other woman Joe had ever known. Of course, as a biological man, Joe hadn't dated any lesbians except Tina. Maybe it wasn't Tina after all, but lesbians who were different. So maybe it was lesbians and not Tina he was falling in love with. He was beginning to realize that he was actually in love with the attention that Tina gave him, not with her.

Things with Tina had been so easy; their relationship had just fallen into place. What's more, Tina thought Joe was a stone butch drag king. A new partner would know, of course, he was a drag king, but would have to learn he was stone butch: not to be touched or probed vaginally. It would be more complicated than it had been with Tina. But at the moment, Joe took little comfort in the fact that he had not actually told these things to Tina, but, instead, she had assumed them about him. He had simply not corrected her; telling himself, with great success until now, that it wasn't a lie, but an omission of the truth. This normally made him feel better.

At five six, Joe had always been short for a man. His petite bone structure, perfectly heart-shaped, full lips, and long curling eyelashes didn't help enforce the masculine image he wished he had, but instead lent a feminine air to his features. This was something Joe had hated most of his life, until that first night he had wandered into Club Kit Kat by accident or, perhaps, providence. He'd had a rough day at work and simply wanted a beer before returning home and going to bed. Kit Kat was conveniently located on his walk home, halfway between the bus stop and his apartment. He'd never paid the corner bar much attention, as he rarely went out, and when he did, Joe preferred to have dinner and drinks with friends at a restaurant, rather than go to a club. But that night, Kit Kat's neon sign called to him, beckoning him to come in. So he did. Paying the two-dollar cover and taking the last empty bar stool at the long bar on the far side of the dark, somewhat dingy club, Joe thought he'd grab a quick beer and head off to bed.

Balancing his briefcase against the bar and foot rail, Joe ordered a draft from the punky, female bartender. He looked around at the cabaret tables in a semicircle facing the small one-foot-high stage with a silver tinsel curtain backdrop. All around the club's fake wood-paneled walls, generic neon signs announced beer brands in harsh, Day-Glo colors. The concrete floor was painted black and in desperate need of a good mopping. On the back wall, a large rainbow flag was hung over what was most likely a window. Rainbow-colored, glittery streamers were draped across the light fixtures suspended from the ceiling. Tacky, Joe thought, taking a sip of his beer. No wonder he had never come here.

The place, he noticed, was full of all kinds of women—sporty women in pullovers with athletic team logos on their chest, women in dresses with high heels, and women in jeans and T-shirts with short, extreme haircuts and, much to his surprise, what his mother lovingly called, "little men." Men who, Joe self-consciously realized, were a lot like him. Short by normal standards and sporting what, in his own sensitivity to social norms, he called a disproportionate number of feminine features. Joe turned back to the bar and sipped his beer, telling himself he was projecting his own insecurities onto the crowd.

He had, after all, just had the worst day of his life. Having worked up the nerve to finally ask MaryAnn from accounting out, she had laughed as if it were a joke. When she realized it wasn't, he had to stand there and watch her recoil as if he had asked her to eat a live octopus, as she told him no. If that wasn't bad enough, after lunch, the major contract he was working on fell through and he'd ended up staying late to attempt to salvage what he could of the relationship with the client. By tomorrow, everyone in the office would know he had asked MaryAnn out and he'd have to face snickers and jabs for weeks. Not to mention that his boss would be angry for months about the lost client.

Joe glanced into the mirror behind the bar to study the reflection of the crowd. He wasn't projecting. The man in the cowboy hat with the handlebar moustache couldn't be an inch over five four, and despite his muscular arms, he was even more slight of frame than Joe. The stocky, blue-collar guy, five seven at best, had the most feminine jawline and nose Joe had ever seen. He was, in fact, almost pretty.

"Are you performing tonight?" a female voice asked the back of Joe's head, pulling him away from his private assessment of the crowd's reflection.

"Me? What?" he asked, spinning the stool around, shocked that a woman was speaking to him, and he was not able to hear her over the music and din of the voices.

The woman smiled. She had shocking red hair. Her large breasts and curves were perfectly displayed in a fitted, black dress with a deep V neckline. When she leaned in close to him the smell of vanilla mixed with a hint of rose filled his nose. Their cheeks were almost touching as she said directly into his ear in a soft voice that cut through the din, "Are you performing in the amateur drag king show?"

"Drag king show?" He had no idea what a drag king was. "No...I..."

"Sorry," she said as she moved away from his ear leaving behind a hint of that vanilla-rose smell. She smiled then shrugged causing her breasts to bounce. She looked him over, moved in closer again and added, "I just assumed. I have to register everyone." She held up the clipboard for him to see as proof of her duties and changed her smile to add a bit of mischief in it. "You look great, by the way. Just fab."

Joe had thought she was fetching even before she had told him he looked great. "Thanks," Joe said, feeling the color rise in his cheeks, unaccustomed to this type of attention from women. "I'm Joe."

"Tina." She offered her hand. He shook it, feeling skin like silk.

"It's nice you dressed up for the event. Usually only the people performing do."

Joe nervously grinned, "Yeah, I just came to watch. It's my first time here."

"Welcome. We do this every Wednesday night." She handed him a flyer as she spoke. "Maybe you will perform next week." Her smile had made him want to perform for her. "I've got to register all these kings! After the show there's dancing. If you're still here, maybe we could dance."

"Yeah, I'd like that. I have to work early tomorrow, but if it isn't too late..." Joe said, wishing he had stopped after yes.

"Great. It was lovely to meet you."

Joe grabbed her hand. Even now he wasn't sure why or where the impulse had come from. He lifted it to his lips like he had seen so many men in movies about the 1800s do, and said, "No the pleasure was all mine, Tina, I assure you." Then he kissed it gently before letting it go.

Tina smiled. "See you later. If you have to leave early, my email is on the flyer. Email me, if you want. Maybe we could have coffee."

"I will," Joe called out, watching Tina's full, curvaceous body swing just slightly from side to side as she walked over to the cowboy.

On the quarter-page flyer, above a line drawing of a tough construction worker with his arms crossed over his chest, block letters proclaimed *Man About Town Drag King Show, followed by dancing with DJ Snatch; Wednesday nights, Club Kit Kat; $2.* Tina's email was printed at the bottom of the page. Joe folded it in half and slipped it into his wallet. Whatever a drag king was, Joe was determined to become one.

And that's how it had started—by accident, by chance. Joe hadn't intended to deceive or hurt anyone. But everything had somehow gotten so complicated. He had been having so much fun; he hadn't even noticed it until he could no longer ignore it.

Joe had always felt somehow different from all of the other men he knew. It wasn't just that he was shorter than most of them, but inside he had felt as if he was wired differently. Joe hadn't ever thought of himself as a girl in a boy's body, and still didn't. He didn't feel like a woman; more correctly, he felt unlike a man. He had never been able to verbalize how he felt, not even to himself, but the new life he'd found at the Kit Kat had opened up a whole world with a vocabulary that made it possible for him to begin to conceptualize his long-felt feelings of discomfort. As it turned out, Joe wasn't a man or a woman. He was a drag king.

Sure, Joe wasn't what he seemed to be. But then no one at the Kit Kat was what he or she seemed to be. Here were women who wanted to be men, women who pretended to be men by performing drag, and women who were actively changing their sex to male—not just cosmetically like the kings, but physically with surgery and hormones; here were also women who looked like cover girls, but only dated other women, and women who looked like dykes who dated other women, and women who looked like guys who only dated other women who looked like guys. In all the perceived confusion, Joe was only a man pretending to be a woman pretending to be a man so he could date a woman who only dated women. *Trans* wasn't the right term for how he felt either.

Joe tried to wrap his head around all of this. If a woman was becoming a man and had sex with a woman who was a lesbian, was it heterosexual sex? More importantly, if he had sex with a lesbian while he was in drag as a drag king was it lesbian sex? And if he had sex with one of these new men, was he a fag? Joe had never been sexually attracted to other men, but there was something about the kings and tranny boys that turned him on. He hated admitting it, even to himself, but there it was.

After all, when he was moving through the world as a man, women paid him no attention. Now here at the Kit Kat they were practically throwing themselves at him as he moved through the world as a drag king. They begged him to date them, fuck them and love them. So why couldn't he be a drag king? How does anyone, after all, become a drag king? Maybe, exactly like he did; with a little research on the Web, a few books, props, and trial and error. Why couldn't he be a lesbian, if he loved women as a drag king? Surely Tina would understand all of that?

Joe exhaled deeply.

Lying on his bed alone, he didn't believe she would. In fact, he knew she'd break up with him if he told her, then she'd tell everyone he was a man. His happiness—a happiness he had never thought possible; the camaraderie he shared with the other kings and the community he'd become a part of over the last four months, would all vanish. Poof, into thin air. The other kings would no longer accept him and might even beat the hell out of him. He wouldn't be able to show his face at the Kit Kat. He wouldn't be able to perform. He would also lose Tina.

He'd have to find a way to smooth this over or he'd have to break up with her.

By Wednesday of the next week, Tina still hadn't returned any of his calls. Joe got ready for the drag show. His ritual was second nature by now. After showering, he tucked his cock back between his legs then plastered on the tight-fitting panty that held his dick in place—a trick he had learned from a drag queen website. The first few times he did this, his cock felt uncomfortable, but Joe got used to the new location of his dick. Now he felt uncomfortable if it was anywhere else. He stepped into the harness and jostled it over the panty, then placed the pack-and-play through the O-ring and pulled each strap until everything was firmly in place, exactly like the woman at the sex toy shop had explained to him.

Joe had been terrified by the idea of going into the sex shop to buy these items. He had walked around near it for over an hour before the cold had forced him to either go inside or leave. Having already invested so much time in the venture and desperately in need of things if he was going to continue his new identity as a drag king, he forced himself to go ahead. He'd been seeing Tina for almost two weeks and had been stalling their first time having sex.

The young woman at the counter greeted him without as much as a bat of the eye. No one rushed over and pointed a finger at him screaming, "He's a man, get him out of here." Nor did any of his other nightmarish fantasies about what was going to happen actually happen. He browsed at the video section, attempting to look nonchalant, but unable to read any of the information printed on the boxes because he was so nervous. As his heart started to slow down, he ventured into the vibrator section where he looked but didn't touch anything for fear it would start to buzz and draw attention. In the book section, he started to feel more comfortable. Books were, after all, familiar to him. He selected *The Drag King Book* and *The Whole Lesbian Sex Book*. With these in his arms, he walked with what he hoped looked like confidence over to the dildo and harness section.

Joe was immediately astonished by the selection of dildos. The sizes, shapes and colors made his jaw drop. The variety of sizes, ranging from pencil thin to mammoth, impressed him, but when he added the shapes from lifelike to twisted in the form of Godzilla, he couldn't believe women would need this many options. On the wall were harnesses displayed on plastic pelvises and below them on a shelf were flaccid and semihard cocks complete with balls in a vast selection of varied flesh tones and lengths. This was what he had come for. He'd learned about this from a drag king website a week ago. He had done some quick research to figure out what to do to have sex as a drag king.

After the last customers in the store left, Joe finally asked the clerk to help him. On her advice, he selected a washable harness made of nylon for easy cleanup and a pack-and-play, which in theory allowed him to pack a softy then flip it around for insertion into a partner. What Joe discovered later was that he needed an actual hard dildo to fuck a woman properly, and, what's more, Tina liked different sizes—different lengths and thickness—at different times. He still preferred the semifirmness of the pack-and-play for packing when he was in drag. It created a semihard, semiexcited bulge in his pants that Joe imagined was hotter than a soft cock, and it had sentimental value being the first dildo he had fucked Tina with. But now he always kept a hard dildo in his bag for after the show.

It was almost time to leave for the Kit Kat. Joe wanted to arrive late, but before the show started. He pulled on the close-fitting boxer briefs, then his Levi's, rolled at the ankles to expose his white bobby socks. Joe wrapped an ace bandage around his chest. He put on a white tank top with a white T-shirt over it, black Doc Martins, and a plain black belt with a big buckle. Joe shaved carefully so as not to cut himself. He didn't have a lot of facial hair, a fact he was never happy about until recently. With a makeup brush he dusted his face with brown eye shadow to simulate a five o'clock shadow. He slicked back his hair in a pompadour of sorts, looking at himself in the full-length mirror. Joe felt like a modern-day James Dean: a rebel without a cause. He'd never, in all his life, thought he'd ever feel like his hero, James Dean.

What would Tina say if he told her the whole truth?

When Joe arrived at the club, Titillating Tom Teaser and Dick Desperate, his closest drag king friends, and their girlfriends, Stacy and Ann, were already at a table. Joe scanned the club for Tina and her clipboard, but she was not there. Tom, who was about Joe's height but thirty pounds heavier, was dressed as a suave 1950s lounge host, complete with a blue sharkskin jacket and matching tie. He was a regular favorite at the club. As soon as he saw Joe, he jumped up and went over.

"Hey, come join us at the table," Tom said, placing a hand on Joe's arm. Joe made eye contact with him. "She's not here. She called Ann and asked her to register everybody. Said she was sick." Tom squeezed Joe's arm making him realize that Tina had said more than that to Ann. Joe nodded. The two of them walked over to the table.

Dick, dressed as a cowboy, pulled up an extra chair and placed it between his own and Tom's as they approached. "Glad to see you," he said, rapping the seat of the chair for Joe to sit down. "I was just running to the bar, could I get you a beer?" Dick was extra thin and tall, lanky with wispy blond hair.

"Sure," Joe said reaching for his wallet.

"On me, man. You get the next one." Dick playfully punched Joe's arm before heading off to the bar.

"You performing tonight?" Stacy asked, bumping Tom with her elbow. "Ann's got the sign-up sheet." Ann looked at Tom then pushed the clipboard toward him without stopping her storytelling.

"Thanks, hon," Tom said, rolling his eyes.

"No. I'm just going to watch," Joe replied. "I don't feel up to it."

"Not feeling well? Maybe you have what Tina has," Stacy said.

Before Joe could answer, Dick returned with beers for the

table. Ann and Stacy went back to their discussion and Tom and Dick talked about a new king who had performed well last week. Joe sat between them all, in silence, lost to his thoughts.

Maybe he should just leave. The tension at the table was almost unbearable. He could go home or pick up some flowers and go to Tina's apartment. He could attempt to patch this up. But what could he offer her to make it better? Or he could just break up with her. Maybe he could get Tom or Dick alone and tell them about the fight. He couldn't be the only stone butch in the room. Maybe someone could give him some advice on how to smooth this over with Tina. Before he could act on any of his plans, the MC took the clipboard from the table and walked up to the microphone.

Joe got up and headed to the bathroom. For show nights, the Kit Kat covered the normal male/female door signs with KINGS and NOT-KINGS signs made of paper. He went into the King's bathroom. Standing over the sink, he looked at his reflection in the mirror. Joe felt sick to his stomach. He splashed cold water onto his face and pulled a paper towel out of the dispenser. He looked more closely into the mirror, remembering his makeup too late, the paper towel in hand and water dripping off his face.

"Blot it," Jack, a pre-op FTM who was a regular at the club, offered from behind Joe. "Don't wipe it, you'll fuck up your beard. Just pat it." Joe hadn't moved so Jack took the paper towel out of his hand and dabbed at Joe's face. "See, no smudges."

"Thanks." Joe looked in the mirror once again and started to dab at more water spots.

"Bad night?" Jack asked, washing his hands in the next sink.

"Bad week."

Joe could see Jack's reflection in the mirror as the king dried his hands. He was checking out Joe's ass. Joe turned around and made eye contact. Jack shrugged and tossed his used paper towel in the trash while walking toward the door.

"Want to get out of here?" Jack asked.

Joe knew what Jack meant. For a second, he thought of Tina, then of Jack. "Yeah, I live a few blocks from here."

"Great. Let's go."

They walked in silence to Joe's apartment. He unlocked the door to let them in. Jack pushed the door closed with a bang behind them. He grabbed Joe by the arms and slammed him against it. For a minute, Joe thought he was going to be beaten up, but then Jack sunk against him. The boy kissed him hard on the lips with an open mouth and ground against his pelvis. Joe kissed him back.

"I knew you liked boys," Jack said as he released Joe.

Joe smiled awkwardly. His mind was spinning. Did he like boys? Jack was after all pre-op, so he was technically physically a girl. Of course, Jack was more of a guy than he was himself. But then, he was a real guy, except he was a girl dressed as a guy, as far as Jack knew. "The bathroom's over there," Joe said, pushing the confusion out of his mind. "I'll meet you in the bedroom."

Jack took his backpack with him into the bathroom. Once the door was shut, Joe rushed to the bedroom, undid his jeans, and slipped the pack-and-play out of the harness. He tossed it into the nightstand drawer where he retrieved the eight-inch black dildo. Unsnapping the bands that held the O-ring, Joe replaced it with a larger one to accommodate the bigger dildo. He stepped into the harness before rebuttoning his jeans. His heart was pounding and his hands were shaking. Jack appeared seconds later, the bulge in his pants substantially bigger.

Jack grabbed Joe and pulled him in. Their sleek muscular bodies seemed at odds with each other, struggling for domination as their tongues explored each other's mouth. Joe could feel Jack's hard cock against his leg. It turned him on, and confused him. He wondered if Jack would let him fuck him in the ass or if Jack would let him fuck him in the cunt. And Joe worried that Jack would want to fuck him.

Jack grabbed Joe's hair and pushed him to his knees. Joe was at eye level with Jack's bulge as the boy undid his belt and pants. Joe had never sucked cock before and he was a mix of nerves and excitement. Jack pulled his hard cock from the pocket of his tighty-whities. It was at least eight inches long with a raised vein and circumcised head. "Suck it," Jack ordered as he hit either side of Joe's face gently with his cock.

Joe licked the tip then gingerly took the head into his mouth. *Does this mean I'm a fag?* At first, he felt as if he'd choke on the cock. He wasn't sure if this was because he was unaccustomed to sucking cock or if he was having a physiological reaction to the act itself. *I want this, don't I?* Joe adjusted to the feeling of the dildo in his mouth and slowly started to work his way up Jack's cock with each inward slide.

"That's a good boy. Take your cock out and work it with your free hand," Jack instructed Joe.

He awkwardly undid his pants and pulled his own dildo from his boxer briefs while still keeping Jack's cock in his mouth. Joe worked his dildo with his right hand as he held Jack's in his left and continued the in and out motion with his mouth. He wanted to please Jack. He was turned on and freaked out at the same time. *Is Jack a girl or am I? Are we both guys? Am I gay, or what?*

Joe gagged and Jack eased off on his thrusts.

"Suck it, Joe. Take more of my cock in."

Joe, excited by the order, tried. Jack's hips started to pump in and out with the rhythm of Joe's strokes.

"Let me fuck your face hard. Take it, boy," Jack grunted into the air.

Joe let go of his fears. Driven by the verbal descriptions, he increased the speed and force of his strokes on both his cock and Jack's. *Fuck it. Who cares what we are?* His body relaxed into the pleasure of the fuck.

"What the hell!" Tina's familiar voice screeched from the doorway. Joe dropped his own cock and pulled away from Jack, whose hips thrust in the air one last time before he realized what was happening. They were both exposed as they looked at Tina and she looked at them. "You're kidding me," Tina said as she turned and ran down the hallway. Joe got up and ran after her, tucking himself in.

"Tina," he shouted as he reached the living room. She was at the door.

"If you are going to fuck someone, at least lock the door."

Joe saw the bottle of wine and flowers on the counter. "What are you doing here?

"I went to the club," Tina said turning around with tears streaming from her eyes. "They said you had left so I came over to apologize. I wanted to say that none of it mattered." She shook her head. "Apparently I don't matter." She opened the door.

"Can't we talk? I want to explain what happened."

"You could have just broken up with me." She stepped into the outside hallway and shut the door.

Joe stood there as if at any moment she would reappear. Instead, Jack emerged from the bedroom with his coat on and his backpack over his shoulder. His big bulge was gone.

"Hey, I'm going to go," Jack said kissing Joe's neck. "I left my number by your bed. When things calm down, call me."

Joe nodded. Jack left.

"Wait," Joe yelled and grabbed the flowers from the counter. He ran into the hallway. Jack was at the top of the stairs ready to go down. Joe hurried to him and held the bouquet out, "Take these. A beautiful boy like you should have them."

Jack took them. They both smiled. Joe watched Jack go down the steps and out into the night.

STRIPPED

Anastasia Mavromatis

It is written. My family adores the phrase, sprinkling it over every expired relationship and personal disaster. It was written that I should flee the family home and reside with strangers, just as it is written for me to perennially incur my father's wrath. To my family, I was the changeling, born into the incorrect family or as my father said, the personification of a divine punishment; he must have done something terrible to receive a daughter who'd lie and defy his authority by having her back etched with ink at the age of eighteen.

Alone in the sunroom, I stare at a finished canvas, fantasizing about the men within the remainder. I belong here as I did on the day of my arrival....

"What do your parents think about this, Alexandra?" Anthony asked, peering through a pair of rimless spectacles.

"About?" I drew my knees together. I needed to pee.

"You sharing a residence with three men."

Damon's blue eyes met mine. Tobias interrupted by asking me whether I took sugar in my coffee, and Anthony waited.

"Well?" Anthony frowned.

"Look, we're busy as it is. We don't have time to wrestle with frantic parents and ethnic concerns," Tobias stated while Anthony turned to eye his friend with surprise.

"Ethnic?" I replied. If that were supposed to offend, he'd have to try harder. "If everything is different to what you're accustomed to, it's ethnic," I spat and it was intentional. I needed to live away from my family home, be away from my dad and his Cretan outlook.

"We have no qualms about that. You seem a splendid candidate."

I adopted the logical male view. "It's either a yes or no, guys."

Tobias, at that moment, graced us in a pair of close-fitting ancient jeans and a ragged tank top, more resembling a bricklayer than an internationally renowned photographer.

"You are aware of our confidentiality clause?" It was Tobias, bending over the coffee table. The four coffee mugs were deposited on four matching coasters.

I nodded.

The clause, which I read just before Anthony returned from work, stipulated the standard expectations of such agreements. See no evil, hear no evil and speak no evil summed up their three page document, which I had to sign and return.

I eventually lugged my luggage through the hall and individually, up the stairs while the others were at work. My room, the converted sunroom on the first level of the old terrace house, was blessed with a partial view of the harbor. The house, of yellow-brown sandstone, in its previous life was once occupied by an English official who was also Anthony's great-great-great-grandfather. The room, vast and tinged with a sweet-sour musty smell that diffused through the walls, would serve as a studio.

The first night was spent lounging on the plush black leather sofa watching satellite TV. After laughing at Brit comedy, I poured myself a glass of Coke and wandered into my room. Unzipping my leather portfolio, I examined my last set of sketches. I baptized the series *Nobodies* as they featured people seen in passing, sitting at bus stops and eating lunch in the city. The inspiration to draw or paint dwindled at home. My parents scoffed at my chosen path, suggesting fruitful occupations that would give me enough clout to impress a potential (and good) family-in-law. During my first year in college, studying art, I'd reject every potential suitor, including those who'd make their way from the old country. I'd reject them all. In my parents' eyes, I was intact. My muse, squashed up against the wall or suffering the equivalent of an anxiety attack, begged me to do something to change the status quo. Announcing my new plans threw my destiny up in the air. Dad exploded. Mother looked at his face and knew she'd have to transform into a Mata Hari of sorts to remain in contact with her daughter.

"You will not speak to this child. She is no longer welcome to my house."

"Yes, Joseph" my mother nodded, rubbing her eyes with a delicate Kleenex until it fell apart.

Dad's words haunted me a little but I looked on the positive; it wasn't as terrible as Kazantzakis's story *Zorba the Greek*, in which the doomed female character falls in love with the foreigner, pushing her unrequited lover to kill himself. It sealed her fate when the grieving father slit her throat. It wouldn't be me, but people thought terrible things when my dad's heritage was laid out on the table like a fake alien.

We did not date.

We did not have sex outside of marriage.

If our partners died, we were destined to live out our life in black.

It was as though he originated from the Dark Star. He ended up with my mother after her father sold him to her via a photograph in the late fifties. The decision was made to bring him to the land of hope, and even though he achieved a lot—thanks to his dowry—he still thought the rest of the world, including the West Coast, would bend to his will. His daughter didn't talk to strange men, let alone share a residence with them, and if she slept with someone other than her intended, he'd be better off dead. And that was the great thing about America; I wasn't limited to the slim pickings within the neighborhood. I fucked outside my ethnic group. Who'd know?

"I'm back. Did you settle in all right?" the voice climbed the stairs and entered my room. Damon leaned against the door.

"Great, no problem whatsoever."

"Okay?" he said. "If you're interested in coffee, I'm putting a fresh pot on now, Allie. You don't mind me calling you Allie?"

I shook my head. It was a first, but I didn't mind.

I followed, like a new pet seeking approval or a new kid in school.

Once we were firmly ensconced with our cups, Damon asked me what I thought of the dating game.

"Don't..." I replied, rolling my eyes. I'd never dated, merely scored in secret: via the Internet or in parked cars during family weddings.

"I agree. It's hideous!" he exclaimed, and this, the green light, dominated the conversation. "It was all flowing rather well. Indeed, I thought Hilda to be one of the most elegant creatures on campus but now..." He shook his head.

"That bad?"

"She's a texter. After we finished dinner and made our respective way home, she sent me one of those text messages." He slid his cell phone across the table.

Njoyed ur company damon lets do it again. U R GR8.

"I see what you mean," I said, replacing the phone on the dining table.

Damon shook his head, "I'm going to have a shower and read. Thanks for listening." And I was great at that—listening.

Whether intentionally or due to absentmindedness, I waited for the deluge to end before I walked past the bathroom. Damon, in a hurry to bathe, had left the door wide open and my first glimpse of his naked body startled me.

When he had first returned from the disastrous date, his body had been covered with a loose shirt that did nothing to define his broad sculpted deltoids. His baggy chinos didn't hint at the plush, firm derriere I now saw. I backed into the hall, and bit into the rising urge to peek. He soaped his stomach and continued to travel south, which I thought nothing of until he stopped to grab hold of his penis. *Penis* is such a drab word, but that's what I'd thought of his genitals up until this moment. As I stood, watching each slow smooth gliding motion of his hand, his penis transformed into a majestic cock, the kind of cock that could have belonged in a skin flick.

Back in my room, every muscle in my body contracted. The electric surge, the backflow of my climax, paralyzed my limbs. My soaked fingers slid away from my spent clit, and my mouth hung open to release the pressure in my head. A sketch pad and a stick of graphite lay by my side, and my reproduction of Damon in the shower, complete with soaring erection, stared back at me.

Damon's body flitted through my mind. I had drawn his contours with the awe of a traveler to a foreign land. My ears had flamed with every stroke. My pulse had quickened and a surge of warmth had flooded my pelvis, taking my cunt to the outer limits. As my hand roamed to the dampening patch of fabric between my legs, I had implicitly known that my image of Damon would change from that point onward. It had been far too sweet to stop. A long-lost stirring had erupted between my thighs, indeed within my womb. I rewound back to the first time I discovered solo pleasure where each butterfly-like flutter within my clitoris paved the way uphill to a jittery climax. The final step, the near blinding electrical impulse, had upturned my toes until my calves cramped.

I found Damon seated at the end of the expansive dining table. He greeted me with a smile before trailing off about Tobias and the most recent global concerns. I sat, poured myself a cup of lukewarm coffee and shrugged, noting the amazing merging of green and blue in Damon's eyes.

Damon chewed on his lip and his long index finger ran through each line on the front page. "I don't know why he bothers." He eyed the newspaper headlines. "Look at that, Tobias will probably end up in Iran one of these days, reporting on the rising tension and before you know it...enough of this," he shook his head. "Tobias arrives at LAX this morning. Want to come?"

Come? The word aptly matched Damon's shower trip. *I'd like to come,* I thought, and gulped down my coffee but instead, "I've a half-finished painting to work on," came out.

The weeks unfolded normally, with the exception of Tobias's quietude. Whether it was to watch the latest DVD or putter about in the garden, his quiet demeanor heavily contrasted with

Anthony and Damon's lurid jokes. Two weeks after Tobias's return, Damon shrugged his shoulders and offered me the short version, his blue-green eyes flickering oddly. "He's always like this when he returns. Sometimes I think he feels guilty about being back in the land of the living."

"Ditto," offered Anthony, seated opposite.

"You can't blame him. I wouldn't be able to talk after being the thick of barbarism."

"Damon, you overdo it, you know?" Anthony smirked.

"I overdo it?"

"Yes, you overdo it. Even Tobias takes it all in his stride, and he's the one who boasts of the scars on his body."

"Like Jesus?"

"Okay, guys," I said, slightly overwhelmed.

"How's your work coming along, Allie?" Damon's changing of the subject put me on the spot. The only work I had completed was the usual housework. It was part of the arrangement, which worried my girlfriends. They launched their ideology, disagreed with my subservience and failed to understand that by swapping my nine-to-five office job for "housework" and other domestic duties, I also had more time to pursue my art.

"I'm stuck at the moment so it's all about randomness. Sketching nothing really," I said, directing my gaze toward my fried eggs.

"You'll get there," Anthony said, smiling kindly.

Damon and Anthony finished and left, one to a dental appointment and the other to the gym. With Tobias meeting his agent, I had the house to myself.

I eagerly climbed the stairs two steps at a time and found myself on the threshold of Tobias's orderly world. His bedroom, quaintly decorated with his photographs of foreign strangers, featured a neatly made king-sized bed. His bedside drawers, stripped of books, photo frames and bedside lamps, were freshly polished so that the red-brown timber glistened. Swallowing another gulp of air, I entered and felt part of his world. I'd taken the chance to examine his work just before his return. All the major think-tank magazines carried his photo stories, images of sadness, terror, blood, panic, disease, all draped with the curtain of disenchantment. Safe behind his camera, his life behind the lens as he looked through a limited field offered him a small degree of distance for the fraction of shutter time. Then he'd walk through districts that I'd imagine, and essentially think where to walk, if it was safe and whether or not he'd have time to catch a quick bite.

"You looking for something?"

Funnily enough, my body didn't twitch. His voice, to my ears, sounded distant. I swiveled from my waist and saw Tobias leaning against the doorjamb. Words trickled through my mind but they keeled over before they could exit my mouth. I shook my head. He walked through, aiming for the left bedside drawer. It was after he pulled out a flannel shirt, his usual gardening attire, that I felt the tide of embarrassment filling the capillaries. I felt myself glowing hot from the bungled moment.

I was within my body, but without. My eyes registered him pulling up his T-shirt. His lean tan back drew my mind closer. Skin, smooth yet tortured, faced me. A jagged scar ran from his left shoulder blade to his waist. Tobias turned and explained it all with the precision of a physician. "It's from a serrated knife, one strike and he carved into my trapezius muscle. Yugoslavia 1990…"

My eyes were busy following a crater, the size of an apricot, on the same shoulder.

He averted his eyes and his face reddened. Farther down, just before his navel and an inch toward the left were scald marks.

His entire physique resurrected my eighth-grade physical education teacher and her favorite "You've been in the wars" phrase that I didn't dare utter. Despite his unease, my curiosity grew. Did he have other scars? Did they influence his intimate life? My only thought, as odd it as it felt, pertained to kissing and licking his scarified flesh.

For months I'd been sitting on a raft and for the same period of time the raft and I sat in a still river. Standing in front of Tobias, who ran a finger to nervously groom his black hair, the current arose to strike me from within.

Man and body, body and man.

"I'd like you to be my subject." It flew out of my mouth and toward him with the rapidity of a hummingbird.

His eyes calmly absorbed me while his ears absorbed the suggestion. The compulsion to touch him at that instant was too overpowering to ignore. Less than a foot way from him, I paced, like curious feline. His scent, a mix of soap and his own natural odor, woke my taste buds. I wanted to taste every morsel of his flesh, to suck, lick, ingest...

The wetness on my lips alerted me to the unfolding kiss, its random origin and fire. Moisture coated my mouth; his tongue began its exploration. Each calm second stripped away each forthcoming moment so that my feet felt separate from the floor and although my hands clutched his shoulders, I felt removed from the reality of our oral expedition. Tobias's mouth closed in, his lips engulfed my tongue. A long slow feeding process followed, his lips pressed against my bottom lip to draw it out, tug it forward so that the warm wet tip of his tongue could skate along the inner lining. A wet wrestle followed our lingual sword fight and after the miniwar, our feeding continued. It was as though our tongues were engaged in their own oral orgy, indulging and imbibing so much more than what was anticipated. He grasped my hand and slowly ran it down his chest, over his belly. I looked up to see his eyes flame over.

"You're here now...hold my cock," he said, finishing with a hoarse grunt.

There I stood wanking Tobias, another Eve in the garden, my vulva glowing hotter by the second. Between my legs, another waterfall stirred. Each cataract gushed like a warped fountain, splashing here and there. I could only do what came naturally; direct his hand to my cunt until I felt his fingers peel me apart. Deeper, stronger and bolder, I tore my mouth away from his to look at his rotating wrist. His two digits worked into me; snug and coated with the fluid of my fascination, arousal and hunger, they curled against my soft flesh.

He slipped out of me, raised his hand to his mouth and licked a second helping. If I didn't collapse, then I'd slip on my very own puddle.

"You're in trouble, Allie. You know it. I know it. There is no way back...not now."

The door clicked shut. My delayed reflexes operated on the moment that unwound between Tobias and me. My eyes searched the floor, simply to gain equilibrium.

What was unfolding?

The question dissolved as quickly as it formed. His eyes searched my face but his hands confirmed his intent. Warmth from the pressure of his hands embraced my wrists. His perspiration and desire entwined, entering my mouth through his breath. His searching lips pressed against my mouth and my tongue automatically slid out to meet his flesh. Much like in a dream, where my sluggish feet failed to pick up speed, arousal and curiosity overruled my logic. Leading me toward the bed, like a professional dancer, he positioned me on my knees. His hand dived between my legs, hastily upturning the fabric of my skirt.

Exposed, an understatement, as the fabric of my skirt bunched up around my waist, I felt his fingers return to the sticky oasis.

"Oh..." I raised my hips, slightly rattled. Back and forth, like riding an invisible stallion, I backed into his hand, drawing him deeper into me. The silent sun swam through the curtain slit, illuminating my arms and for a few seconds I create two elaborate tattoo sleeves for my virgin arms.

Tobias, intoxicated with the aroma coming from my sex, grunted and slid out. It was a short interruption, enabling him to strip off the remainder of his clothes before returning and balancing my neck between his thumb and forefinger.

"I'm going to fuck you," he whispered. He removed his hand and threw me onto my back. "I want to see." He knelt between my thighs, parting them before raising them up to my hip joint.

"That's nice," he said, running his fingers over my swollen labia.

"Stop teasing and do it. I want it." Surprised by my alacrity, I fixed my eyes on his damp chest and bit my lower lip until blood slid down my throat. His plump and rigid prick rubbed against my pubic mound. Tobias returned my smile and grasped the base of his shaft, slowly sliding himself over my clit. His slow invasion of cock drove out my breath. Its implicit neediness filled me with an eagerness that I only once before knew. The interval between trysts can make one conveniently forget the sensation of being filled. Lingering around the wet entrance to exacerbate my anticipation, he watched my face. His mouth fell open in time with my own mouth and his hips automatically followed through, striking my pelvis as he ground his cock into me. We danced like this for moments, until the angle of sunlight altered and my legs wound around his waist. The tempo of the fuck varied. Deep, shallow, fast and slow; he felt pleased and so did I. At each turn I felt alive and the specter of insatiability draped our bodies. Prying my labia apart, he viewed the slick river between my legs and remarked on the heat that wrapped around his cock. Our lips met, as did our tongues. The purpose of the kiss didn't dawn until I felt him slide out and his mouth take a detour, planting a wet trail from the hollow of my neck to the apex of my flooded labia. Anguish filled me like cake icing, as did his tongue, swirling, tickling my slit. His eyes briefly returned to mine before addressing an incoming shadow.

If you fell from a building, traveling too fast to clutch on a passing ledge or balcony, then you'd know it was too late to return to your starting place. A new scent entered our scene. I saw Anthony hovering above me. His upside down form unnerved me at first. My perspective altered, as did the encounter. Unperturbed, Tobias continued drinking from my overflowing cunt. Kneeling, Anthony stroked my hair.

"This is quite cosy," Anthony whispered, seducing my ear between soft strokes of his tongue along my earlobe.

His hand lazily stroked my chest.

Even as I swayed within the farthest reaches of my mind, I noticed the growing bulge in Anthony's pants. Tobias changed tack and altered the rhythm with the sturdy entry of his fingers. Filled and expanded, I sighed. Anthony's kiss, rougher than Tobias's, required more energy. His lips gripped my tongue, drew it out and massaged its length, sucking me into a lustful vortex to watch me drown. I reached out, opening my mouth, only for Anthony to rear back and grip my right breast with urgency. Anthony watched Tobias's wrist twist and turn. Their silent communiqué tautened my resolve. Sensing Tobias's retreat, I turned to see him suck his soaked fingers.

Erect and half spent, Tobias smiled and returned his lips to mine.

"Taste it," he murmured, as Anthony parted my legs wider

still. His thumb liberally taunted my vulva, stroking me up and down. Just as Anthony's mouth settled on my mound, the front door slammed shut.

It was like swimming within an underwater cave, desperately searching for an air pocket for survival. Tobias's hungry mouth latched onto my areola and drew it out, until the sensitive area screamed within his warm mouth. Anthony's zipper whirred and his cock sprang forth. Tobias, eager to watch, slid his hand along my abdomen, toward my pussy and opened me up farther so Anthony could see the extent of the elongated torture.

"Do it." It was my own voice that made the request. My lumbar muscles struggled to elevate my torso so I could see his magnificent cock at my entrance. We probably exhaled at the same time. Anthony's hips swayed, his cock glided in and his smile confirmed his internal jubilation. Damon's arrival home did little to quell the insatiable beast within me. Tobias's attempt to muffle my wanton moans failed. My mouth slid away from his.

"Please...harder."

My secretions filled the room. The wet rhythm intensified as his moist balls and pelvis slammed against my groin.

"Come and feel her, Tobias."

They swapped and Anthony knelt over me, his damp cock brushing my lips. Tobias reentered with care and attention to the oral rhythm unfolding a few inches away from him. Licking off my own heady perfume from both men filled me with egoism never before known or anticipated. Anthony's eyes closed as I engulfed his cock and Tobias writhed inside me like a water snake.

Sex and love; love and sex. Definitions unraveled and dissolved.

From the corner of my eye I saw Damon watch my lips glide along Anthony's cock, anointing it with silvery streams of saliva.

Damon took his turn as Anthony pulled me up and onto my knees. I sank into the mattress and stroked the shimmering stream between my labia.

Damon's hands gripped my buttocks. "Fuck, this is nice."

Time evaporated and my need resurfaced; Damon's slathered my ass with my juice, before sliding his middle finger into the tight slit.

His smooth cock followed, and the burst of fire that followed after he entered my ass almost pulled me under. Anthony, in front, squeezed my breasts and failed to distract me from the sizzling heat within my ass. If anything, it aggravated my own sense of uncertainty. On the fence between pain and pleasure, I needed a smooth climax yet desired the agitation of used muscles and a stretched ass.

Damon gently slid in and out, then shoved his cock to the hilt. Tears sprang from the corners of my eyes. My own voice resembled a human-animal hybrid: a wounded deer or an exhausted lioness.

He rocked against me as Anthony's chest blocked my view. Another mouth, Anthony's, met mine as Damon continued his deep, torturous fuck. My skin broke out in gooseflesh as his cock assaulted my ass. Semipartnered by Anthony, his hand gripped mine, making room for Tobias's fingers once more.

"You want to come don't you, Allie?" asked Tobias. Their combined testosterone cradled and tucked me into the blistering fuck, stripping away age-old layers of convention.

A visceral groan answered in the affirmative, but another part of me didn't want it to end in case it all changed and we all transformed into meek drones.

Tobias burrowed into my pussy, fingers aflame, as Damon's pelvis adhered to my rump, burying his cock deeper in my burning ass. My mind didn't stop to consider that Tobias, still full, hadn't climaxed or that Anthony waited for release, I only thought of Tobias's fingers skating over my clitoris and how this activated a gripping chain reaction. From behind, Damon fired off deeply, discharging into me. Tobias continued to work away, his fingers scissoring around my clitoris, gripping it tenaciously as my inner thighs trembled and my brain responded to my cunt with quaking electric pulses. Anthony, directly in front, beckoned me—his eyes did all the talking. My hand gripped his cock like one gripped a handle, and pumped his shaft until his warm load splattered my back. Tobias shuddered as his own hand strangled his cock to a fierce climax after he finished masturbating me.

Tobias was the first to speak as Damon braced his knees like a sprinter, "That was long overdue."

"How do you feel?" Anthony's question opened a door to another confession.

"Feel? I'll be sore later...but—"

"Well?"

The telephone in the hall interrupted the moment. Damon rose to intercept the call.

"I feel like it could be a regular thing...that's if you're not embarrassed." This couldn't be me. Logic took its time, more moments passed and I felt relieved that shame, that ugly social construct, had ceased to exist. Tobias sat next to me and massaged my shoulders.

"I like the way you think," he said.

"I think we could make an arrangement," said Anthony.

As long as I didn't have to sign another confidentiality agreement, I'd be there.

STABLE MANNERS

Lily Harlem

Six Sundays in a row his brooding gaze has scorched from the twilight shadows of the ménage. Black eyes narrowed, expression sulky, he's devoured my body with a fierce intensity as I've struggled to maintain a cool, professional image.

Standing alone as he was, away from the more sociable parents, I initially assumed he was concentrating on his daughter's dressage skills, but before long I realized it was me, her tutor, he was fixating on each week for a full hour and a half.

Now, as I turn my back to watch the trotting ride, I can feel his greedy eyes devouring my jodhpur-encased rear. This knowledge thrills me and makes my hips roll for his enjoyment. I sashay—just a little—as I move through the barky mulch explaining the fineries of smooth transitions. I appreciate his attention, really I do.

I have a spare riding crop stuck into my left boot; it leaves my hands free for adjusting stirrups, tightening girths and gesturing to the letters around the school; it's a quirky habit I've always had. As I'm stepping toward his daughter the slightly pliable rod slaps against my thigh, flicks backward and forward in time with my pace like a musician's metronome. "Here you go, Emily," I say, whipping it out and handing it up to her. "You need to get used to holding a crop even if you're not going to use it." I smile at the pretty ten-year-old as she nods and adjusts it into the grip of her reins.

I throw a glance at her father. His eyes hit me full on, steady and unwavering. Drinking me up like a man dying of thirst. My knees weaken, my ears buzz and my chest tightens. In the otherwise formal, asexual world of dressage he's a refreshing dose of pure, unadulterated testosterone. He looks positively wild; a barely contained stallion, cooperating with his tamer—just.

I wish I'd brought a crate to sit on. Each week he affects my blood flow more and more, reduces my concentration and sends my highly regarded teaching skills into a scatter of nerves. He's so tall, so broad and so damn handsome.

Today he's wrapped in a dense, black winter coat, one gloved hand shoved deep into his pockets whilst the other circles a mug of steaming liquid. Maybe I just imagine him watching me each week. I've never even heard him speak. I only know he breathes because of the plume of cold air steaming around his head like a bad boy's halo. Excitement churns through me at the thought of how bad someone like him could be. What would happen if the hunger pouring from his eyes demanded to be satisfied? What would happen if I was the one to satisfy it? I clear my dry throat and return to explaining the next exercise, try my hardest to focus whilst wrapped in thoughts of sating his appetite.

This final lesson of the day draws to an end and I instruct my six riders to dismount. They lead their horses into the chill of the winter evening, past the dark hay barn and into the long row of amber-lit stalls. As forecasted it's starting to snow, and big, determined flakes float through the weak lights of the yard and settle on the straw-littered cobbles.

It will take half an hour for the juniors to untack their ponies, buckle New Zealand rugs and give the saddles a soap. It's a clever ploy to add "stable management" to the end of the last lesson; the youngsters do what's essentially my job and their waiting parents pay for the privilege. I've added a free coffee machine in the viewing area and no one seems to have cottoned on to my devious, but nevertheless, entrepreneurial idea.

I decide to make the most of this free time and head into the cavernous barn to load nets for the liveries. The sweet scent of hay fills my nose like a wave of incense and I pause at the entrance to let my eyes adjust to the inky darkness. Kids have been playing in here again, mounds of bales have been arranged to form a staggered wall and what looks like a tall castle turret. I smile; it's what they should be doing, who cares if it's not the neatest barn in the world.

My feet are silent as I move to a half-used bale and bend to unhook its tight orange string. It's awkward and with my butt in the air I fumble in the darkness, struggle to release the sharp cord of knots.

Suddenly I'm aware of a long, thin pressure on my left buttock. Firm and solid it presses against the give of my flesh.

My breath snatches. I know exactly what it is.

It's my own crop!

I don't bother to straighten. Instead I twist my torso and see a silhouette standing at my left shoulder. Broad, square shoulders and a mop of wayward curls tower next to me. I should be indignant at the personal, inappropriate touch from someone I don't know, but instead I feel a sudden knot of pleasure rock through my body. After all, I've been fantasizing about this man for weeks.

The chilled skin on my buttock soars to hypersensitivity as the crop continues to exert a confident pressure. A deep roll of excited anticipation lurches in my stomach. He's so close, only feet away. Lining my crop up against me, touching me intimately but at the same time distantly.

He says nothing—neither do I.

After a moment of bending before him I shift my backside a fraction, the smallest twitch of a movement, just to see what he'll do.

The pressure releases, there's a brief hiss in the cold air and then a sting sears through my jodhpurs and onto the delicate skin of my butt. A shard of lightning, a second of sweet torture. It heats my cold flesh and buzzes my pain receptors to life.

A squeak of shock escapes my lips; I can't believe he did what I wanted him to do—I didn't even know I wanted him to do it! My hands curl into the string I was struggling with. He hit me, he's never even spoken to me but he's so self-assured he's gone straight for a kinky, sharp spank. My head floods with excitement; it's been a long time since I felt something new.

I let the heat travel and pool between my thighs, and to my surprise it swells my hidden folds and a pleasurable hum settles in my clit. A thought enters my head that if he treats the other cheek the buzz will multiply. I stay bent over the hay bale, shift slightly and to my delight he takes full advantage of the opportunity. He lines up the crop on my right buttock and my nipples peak to attention beneath my thermal top. I hear it sail through the air and that brief nanosecond between knowing it's coming and the pain of the hit is the most delicious anticipation I've ever known.

I revel in the heated discomfort, lap it up; he's given it so easily. The hum in my clit escalates to a hungry pull and I feel myself turning full on. Who is this guy?

I straighten and face him. He can see my lusty expression because the orange glow from the yard is flowing around me, but he's as black as night to my eyes. Only the rough curls of his hair and the shape of his tall outline are visible. He is perfectly motionless, not even a twitch of the crop that now hangs limp from his hand.

I want more. Much more. No man has ever touched me like that and my desire is so sudden and all consuming that my head is no longer in control of my body.

I neglect my fine leather crop, which I presume he's returning, and step backward into the deeper shadows of the barn. I climb over scattered bales and disappear around the tall turret the children made. I lean my back against the scratchy wall and beat down thoughts of rational, lucid behavior; I don't want them interfering with my moment of revelation.

I wait in the dark silence; the biting cold now a welcome blast to my fevered state. Will he follow me? Did I read it all wrong? Damn, what's going on?

His bulky presence rounds on me, draws up at my side and immediately invades my personal space. It's so pitch black the whites of his eyes are the only thing I can truly make out. That and the heat blazing off his body like a roaring fire.

"Hi," I whisper, my voice husky and needy even to my own ears.

He takes a step closer and I sense him staring down at me, though how he can see I have no idea. After a few, painful, drawn-out seconds, just as I'm about to bolt, my mouth is caught. Hard and urgent his lips press down and his tongue forces mine to part for his delicious invasion.

I melt, open up for him, thoughts of bolting fly from my

mind. He tastes of strong, black coffee, warm and intoxicating. A whirl of male pheromones floods my senses and cranks up my lust level. I let my body lean against his and curl my hands over his shoulders. His coat is rough under my open palms; I want it off, I want to feel him, make sure he's real. I slip my fingers under his collar and shove. He doesn't seem to mind and the weighty garment drops with a whoosh to the hay-filled floor. I return to his marble-hard shoulders and sense a thick woolen jumper covering unnervingly powerful muscles. He could have hit me so much harder. I shiver at the thought.

His arms have locked around my puffer jacket, one secured around my shoulders and the other around my waist, squeezing me tight as he kisses as though his life depends on it. I pull away a fraction, fighting to breathe and his lips dip to my neck, sending a stream of fluttering butterflies across my scalp and down to my aching tits. Damn, he's one hell of a kisser.

He releases me and I miss him instantly. I hear the zipper on my jacket. Fast and urgent it whizzes free and he shoves it to the floor the way I shoved his. The cold doesn't even register; we're creating our own fiery heat in the shadowed depths of the barn.

His hands run down my torso, dip into my waist and over the flare of my hips, travel farther to the raw heat of my still supersensitive buttocks. I let out a little whimper but he silences me with his mouth. Big palms squeeze through my jodhpurs, kneading and massaging the sting; my legs turn to jelly at the reminder of searing pain. I want more.

He seems to sense this because he sinks to the floor and pulls at my riding boots, first one then the other. He pushes to his knees and I can't resist running my hands through his thick hair while he undoes my jodhpurs and rolls them down my legs along with my knickers. With an impatient tug they are removed and my entire bottom half is exposed to the elements. Cool fresh air rushes to meet my hot, private flesh and reminds me where we are. We can't do this, not here. Surely not.

I feel him lift my leg and realize he's pulling my boots back onto my bare calves. A tidal wave of panic spreads over me: What if someone comes? Some kids or one of the parents. What if someone comes and I'm standing in long black boots and a thermal fleece but minus my jodhpurs and underwear? My reputation as the best show tutor in the county will be in tatters!

I wriggle against his determined hands and step back, with every intention of finding my jodhpurs. I need to get them on and make a break for it.

I'm forcefully shoved against the hay and it scratches mean little points into my buttcheeks. "Hey," I protest in a whisper. But then I feel him drop and loosen my thighs with his hands. His cheek presses against the hot skin over my left hip bone. I tremble in his grip and forget about making a run for it. I can barely dare hope what he might do next; how the hell will I stay standing up?

And then he sets to it. With a skillful swirl of his mouth he parts my ripe flesh and his tongue arrows through the soft folds surrounding my clitoris. He catches the hard little nub in a wet kiss and begins a gentle sucking motion. Stars explode before my eyes and I jab my hands onto his shoulders for support, pull in a long, low hiss of air.

I arch my back as his questing fingers search out my juices. I'm so wet for him. His suction releases and his tongue begins to flick over my clit as a cool finger finds my opening. He pushes in and stretches me. I let out a tight sigh and collapse against the hay wall behind me. He adds another finger and they bend within me, hit that supersensitive spot with scary accuracy. "Oh, god, I can't...I can't stand up for this," I moan quietly, as the friction inside becomes overwhelming. I'm close, so close.

Rubbing against my G-spot is making my clit pulse in warning, it's swelling and demanding relief. I drop harder onto him and feel the pressure from his mouth increase. The sizzle of an impending release shoots along my spine. So close. I'm going to come in the barn. So close.

Then he's gone, out, away. I'm empty, alone.

I open my eyes to the blackness, ready to scream with frustration. I was just about to have a raging orgasm and he pulled away. Damn him!

But he's still there, in the shadows, right in front of me. He kisses my mouth to silence my despair and I can taste myself on his lips, musky and feminine—the opposite of him. God, I want to sample his flavor.

Hands spread on my shoulders and he spins me to face the hay tower. He raises my hands above my head and with his foot pushes apart my legs. My body feels boneless with frustration, weak and indignant. I'm at his mercy. I love it.

"More?" he growls, a demand as much as question. Lust drips from his deep voice and I feel the crop press on my bare buttocks. This time there will be no material to soften the blow. I do want more. I want to know what it feels like to be spanked on naked flesh. But can I? Dare I? Here?

"Yes," I plead into a bale. I need to know; it's all I need to know at this moment in time. "Yes."

The crop cracks across my right cheek, hard and sharp, a single blow. Just as I think it doesn't hurt too bad the pain blossoms to a rising heat, getting stronger and hotter. "Ah...ah... ah," I mouth into the hay.

I feel something in front of my face, it's not his lips, it's a glove made of thick fleece material and he offers it to bite on. "Shh," he breathes by my ear.

I nod. I'll be good. No more sounds. I just want him to do it again. I want to feel that heat bloom to my clit and make it pulse and jump some more. A few seconds later another burst of pain breaks right through the first one, then there's a third leathery thwack against my tormented skin. I grip the hay, pull out handfuls and chew down on the glove. I don't like it, I can't stand it. I adore it; I want him to go for a fourth.

He swats at my cheeks again and then aims one for my thighs, the pain changes, endorphins are being released. Now it's all pleasure; every single stroke buzzes me to a wonderfully hypersensitive state. Reality fades and I feel the orgasm calling again. It will take so little to tip me over. He strikes some more, controlled but heated, each hurt a blur as it builds the bigger picture. I reach down and push my hand between my own legs, fumble for a way of releasing the pressure.

"SHERRY... SHERRY...!" A teenage voice breaks through my crazy new world with all the grace of an earthquake. "ARE YOU IN THERE, SHERRY?"

I freeze every bodily function I possess. Even my heart stops beating.

One of the youngsters is in the doorway of the barn. *Shit, shit, shit,* rings through in my head, a mantra of panic. There will be no time to dress or hide if she ventures in to look for me.

She shouts out again. "SHERRY, ARE YOU IN THERE? I THINK ROCKY'S SADDLE IS SPLITTING ON THE POMMEL. CAN YOU TAKE A LOOK?"

Neither of us moves; we don't make a sound, we don't even breathe for fear of discovery. I couldn't care less about a split pommel; all I can think of is my naked ass being beaten in public by a complete stranger.

"Is she in there?" A familiar voice joins the hunt for me.

"No, I don't think so, Emily. She must be down the bottom field."

"Just wait for her to get back; it's too cold to go all that way. You can clean the bridle for now."

"Yeah, I suppose."

To my giddy relief their footsteps drift away and their high-pitched chatter fades.

I drop my hands from the ragged hay and release the glove from my mouth. My arse is on fire, my pussy demands attention, but I can't do this. Not here. Not now. The risks are too great. That was too bloody close.

He apparently has other ideas and before I can utter a word he's on me. His tongue plunges into my mouth and his arms pull me to the floor beneath him. "We can't..." I whimper, fighting to hold on to my thin thread of sanity.

"Shh..." he soothes, his dense weight pinning me to the carpet of hay. Sharp little spikes prod at my bare bottom and the tops of my legs. He kisses me hard and I feel his erection shoving against my naked mound, offering its glorious length and girth even through his trousers, rubbing me, tempting me.

Thinking gives way to feeling.

I kiss him back. We have to get on with this—quick.

He takes the hint and rocks to his heels. I make out his bent shoulders and hear the zip of his flies. Then he's back over me, determined and heavy. He's going to be big and hard and in one hell of a rush. I throb with longing, tremble with anticipation.

But he has other ideas, instead of going for a fast missionary he grabs my legs and folds my knees onto the thick material of the top I'm still wearing. He then loops my booted feet over his wide shoulders and pulls my burning buttocks up onto his bent knees. I let out a whimper of frustration. I need to be filled. Now. I just want him to get on with it in the most efficient way possible. Nothing fancy when we're playing with fire.

He nudges to find my damp opening, takes aim and then in

one sharp thrust buries his penis to the hilt. The whole length of him pushes up against my womb and his width spreads me wider than ever before. I go to cry in pain and delight but no sound emerges. His hand is clamped across my mouth. I can't tell him how good it feels to have his hard wedge of flesh burning me on the inside the same way he's scorched me on the out.

He pulls back a fraction and then shoves in with a barely audible grunt of approval. Totally dominant, perversely confident, he's silk on steel. I can hardly move as he thrusts again and again. He removes his hand from my mouth and sends it to massage the burn on my buttocks. The other finds my clit and he circles and frets as his cock works my internal spot.

I bite hard on my lip, taste a draw of blood. The hay weaves into my hair and clothes as I'm rammed several inches upward and then pulled back down with his demanding thrusts.

Swirls of delicious, greedy sensations pump through my vagina; breathtaking electricity jumps to my clit. The tension builds, grows, mounts, one more hard pound...one more loop of his fingers...and I'll roller coaster over the edge of heaven. I need it now; I hold a breath in tormented anticipation of the explosion.

"What the fuck!" he swears and backs out of me with a slippery jump.

The hay by my ear rustles and my body tenses to the point of actually breaking bones. My legs drop from his shoulders and I feel a pressure land on my chest.

It's the damn stable cat!

"Get the hell out of here," I hiss furiously and push to my elbows to shift his inquisitive body.

"Meow..." He leaps with suitable indignation and melts into the darkness. I can feel erratic heartbeats skipping in my chest; I may well be having a heart attack. "We should stop, this is too close for comfort," I gasp.

Within a second I'm flat on my back and being rammed into again, unable to voice any further opinion. His tongue plunges into my mouth in time with his thrusting hips. My legs are free at his side leaving his pubis perfectly positioned to connect with my clit. Over and over and over he grinds. My hips arch to greet his. This is too good to walk away from. Could a person die of pleasure? Could a person die of shame?

I can feel myself panting, desperate for oxygen. The cold whooshing into my lungs and mixing with the heat of his urgency is the strongest drug in the world. Sweat rises over me and need races across my nerve endings. "Don't," I whisper by his ear. "Don't stop..."

His lips find my neck and he sucks—hard—to the point of more pain and I know he's losing control. Deep within me his cock goes as rigid as any cock can go. He's as near to coming as I am.

"God, yes...yes," he hisses into my hair, his voice harsh and hoarse.

His approval sends me reeling. Heat erupts on my flesh as my eyes flash open to the darkness. A low, guttural moan rumbles to the tip of my tongue only to be devoured by his hot mouth. His hips jerk with unimaginable power as his cock flays my nerve endings into a blissful state of no return. Pleasure overtakes me, holds me high on the precipice between the buildup and the inevitable convulsions, and then, then I let myself fall into oblivion.

His whole body bucks above me and joins me in the same climactic moment of euphoria. "Oh, yes...there, baby, that's good... God, you're so fucking good." It's the most he's ever said to me.

He drives deeper still as his mouth tears from mine and his

shoulder muscles turn to granite. My internal muscles spasm and clench him, squeeze out every second of his orgasm and mix it with my own in a wild caress of joy.

His cheek slides against my face, rough and sharp with stubble. He tries to internalize his primeval groan but doesn't manage. I cushion it in my mouth to keep us as quiet as possible.

His weight slumps, squashes down on me. He's heavy and uncomfortable but I rejoice in his all-consuming exhaustion. The exhaustion I'm responsible for.

The moment doesn't last long; we haven't the luxury of time. All too soon he's up and out, leaving me empty and hollow. But I can still feel him in me, doing his stuff, delighting my insides.

My jodhpurs land in a heap on my lap and he pulls at my boots. With shaking, fumbling fingers I undo the knot of my trousers and knickers and slip them on. He offers his hand and pulls me upright. My heart is pounding so hard I'm sure he can hear it. God, what did we just do? It was foolhardy, irresponsible, kinky and daring. My breathing is barely under control.

I slip into my boots and hunt for my jacket. It's strewn on a bale to the right. I shrug it on and he twines his big fingers with mine, straightens his own heavy coat and runs a hand through his wild hair.

We walk around the turret and into the window of light dribbling in from the yard. At the doorway we stop and look at the fat snowflakes floating silently from the night sky. I don't want to speak and spoil the magic of our postcoital moment. This feels too perfect.

After a full minute he turns to me and says, "I'm Blake by the way." He offers a tilt of his lips, a smile but not quite.

"Sherry," I say, and then feel stupid; he knows my name.

A stampede of wellies suddenly heads toward us. Emily and her friends skid across the yard, snowballs filling their palms and hoots of delight echoing around the stable block. "Hey, Dad, take this," she shouts, hurling a lump of snow through the air.

Blake ducks and it lands inside the barn, missing its target. He straightens and turns to me and I realize it's the first time I've seen his expression anything other than somber. His whole face is alight; he looks happy, alive. Creases gather around the corners of his dark eyes and I notice how white and straight his teeth are as he laughs. He should do it more often, it's infectious.

Still smiling he reaches out and dips his fingers into my hair, retrieves a long piece of hay with a seeded end. He shows it to me briefly before tossing it over his shoulder. "You want to go and get some food?" he asks.

I see a flash in his bad-boy eyes and know it's an offer of wicked dessert rather than a wholesome dinner.

I nod—I'm still hungry.

EQUIPMENT

Kay Jaybee

The moment I saw his naked arse, I knew that I wanted to fuck it, and I told him so. It was the first time I'd seen Lee Cooper unsure of himself. For a split second a veil of uncertainty, possibly even fear, had crossed his generally ultraconfident square features. It didn't last though, and he was soon shrugging my statement off with a lad-ish laugh. "You ain't got the equipment, baby," he said, as he eased his solid cock into my willing body.

I started working part-time at the garage, where Lee is employed as a mechanic, three months ago. The first thing he said to me, as his clear brown eyes appraised my slight frame and red plaited hair was, "I'm looking forward to pulling on those pigtails, honey." From anybody else I wouldn't have taken a comment like that, but somehow from Lee it was okay. He exuded a sort of sexual confidence, and the instant and silent knowledge that eventually we would fuck radiated from his every pore. It would have been foolish of me to deny that unspoken understanding, and I privately looked forward to the day I'd discover if the tattoos that adorned his muscular arms extended to his chest and down his legs.

That was three flirtatious months ago, and it had been fun letting the erotic tension build between us, get more intense as the weeks of inaction ticked by, till finally Lee's resolve had broken. He told me, as he hammered an impatient fist on my front door during his lunch hour, that he'd been changing the oil in a beat-up old car, when he'd realized he couldn't hold out another moment.

After the glorious frisson of the wait, there was always the risk that the reality wouldn't live up to the expectation. I hadn't been disappointed however, far from it.

I smiled to myself as Lee dragged his grubby boilersuit back on, and disappeared down my garden path at a run. His words echoed in my head, "You ain't got the equipment, baby." A wicked twinkle began to shine in my eyes at the prospect of what lay ahead for the unsuspecting mechanic, and speaking across the empty room, I said, "Well, actually, Mr. Lee Cooper, I have all the equipment we could possibly need...."

The thought of his tight arse, of claiming it as my own, of taking control of Lee for a while, and perhaps robbing him of a portion of his macho attitude, grew within me, and I began to lay plans for the temporary domination of this alpha male.

On Lee's next visit, predictably the following lunchtime, I embarked on a mission to both enjoy myself, and to lull him into a false sense of security, neither mentioning how delicious I found his backside, nor my eventual intentions for it. As his calloused hands made their way over my naked chest, pinching my nipples with exquisitely painful squeezes, I groaned with genuine pleasure. Stroking the beautifully toned body that pushed against mine, I relished the sight of the tanned multi-tattooed chest I'd so recently discovered.

It was on Lee's fourth visit that I kept my hands exclusively on his backside, patting it gently, smoothing it and caressing it in a totally nonthreatening way as my new lover pumped himself swiftly in and out of me.

On the fifth visit Lee announced he'd had a dream about tying me up. His face, when I told him that he could do just that, was a picture. I'm not sure if he was more turned on by the fact he could do anything he liked to me, while my hands were secured behind my naked back, or by the feeling of power my helplessness gave him. I suspect the latter. As Lee's warm tongue explored my stomach, and ducked skillfully between my spread legs, I wallowed submissively in the blissful feelings that engulfed me.

During visit number six, a rare after-work encounter, while Lee was both fucking and smacking my arse with stingingly wonderful efficiency, the last few parts of my plan fell into place, and I knew that my need to take his firm neat backside was reaching the point of obsession.

A little over two weeks after Lee had first turned up on my doorstep, I decided the time had come to act. Laying out my sex toys in a neat row near my pillow, I hid them from view with my duvet. Removing the clutter of clothes from the battered old armchair in the corner of my bedroom, I adjusted its position so that it was at the foot of the bed. Then I took off my regular jeans and T-shirt, and put on my tight black Lycra bodice and matching knickers. The caress of the clinging material against my flesh was enough to increase my pulse rate and boot up the arousal I had been so carefully keeping in check.

Lee's distinctive knock on the door came at almost exactly seven o'clock, as we'd arranged. I smiled quietly to myself at his promptness and, wrapping myself in a black silk robe, descended the stairs to collect my unwitting victim.

"Wow, babe," he said, as his appreciative eyes ran over my robed frame, "like the silk." He reached forward, and I allowed Lee to engulf me briefly in his arms, his stubble scratching my cheeks as his mouth came to mine. Then I broke away from his magnetic warmth, holding him at arms' length.

"You like what you see?" I grinned at Lee, my green eyes reflecting into his brown ones. "You want to see more?"

"You bet." He reached out to take hold of the robe's ties, but I stepped back, causing him to frown questioningly. This was not how it went for him. When Lee reached out, he got what he wanted. Usually.

"Not yet, honey. Come with me." I walked toward the stairs, beckoning him teasingly over my right shoulder.

Seconds later Lee was following me up the stairs like a faithful hound trailing his mistress. *Excellent.* I didn't look back again, but strode purposefully into my bedroom, only stopping when I reached the foot of the bed. When I turned to face him, hands on hips, I regarded Lee sternly, hoping that my mask of authority wouldn't slip.

Lee's expression was one of total confusion as he watched me. I undid my robe, letting it slide provocatively to the floor. Again he stepped forward to touch, but I dodged out of reach. He opened his mouth to protest, but I held up my hand, and spoke first.

"We've had a lot of fun together, honey. We've played it your way, and it's been fantastic. Now it's my turn to call the tune."

"Your turn?" He spoke as if the idea was totally foreign to him, and I suppose it probably was. I can't imagine that any woman would have told Lee what to do before.

I remained calm, stifling my need to breathe deeply and dispel some of the tension that had built up in my stomach. "That's right, my turn. So, take off all your clothes."

"I…"

"All your clothes, Lee. Now. I won't ask you again," His hands rose toward his top, and then he hesitated, so I continued, "Unless you'd rather leave, of course."

Lee stared at me for a few more seconds, as if trying to decide if I was serious or not, and then, with a "What the hell" shrug, he pulled off his T-shirt, dirty jeans, navy boxers and socks. The moment he was naked, I pointed to my armchair. "Sit down."

Again he hesitated, but as curiosity got the better of him he sat, perched on the very edge of the seat. I stood just out of reach of his hands, which still hadn't quite got the message that they weren't allowed to touch. "This is my game, okay?"

Lee nodded, ruffling his fingers across his short spiked, brown hair.

"Good," I walked to the head of the bed, and reaching a hand beneath my duvet, produced a blue silk tie. Lee's eyes widened in both surprise and uncertainty, as I said, "Your hands, please."

He presented his arms to me, his wrists together, as if he were a criminal awaiting the captivity of handcuffs. I began to wonder if he'd had that experience for real. I knew there was a lot of past crammed into his thirty-one years. Holding his gaze for a moment, I ordered him to stand so I could secure the tie firmly around his wrists.

Ripples of power begin to course through me as I saw his impressive body tower over me, his ink-stained chest partially hidden by his tethered arms. Lee's cock, which had been rigid since he'd undressed, was pointing at me accusingly, and I swallowed back the urge to kneel before him and lap at its salty sweet flavor. Instead, I pointed back to the armchair. Understanding my intention, he sat.

Flicking my single neatly plaited pigtail behind my neck, and locking my gaze to his, I began to run my hands over my stomach, neck and arms. Lee licked his lips. His obvious enjoyment of what I was doing spurred me on to slip a first tentative hand toward my crotch. As I was lingering over the narrow waistband of my black panties, I heard Lee take a sharp breath, and I smiled as he unconsciously leaned forward in the chair, his arms tugging a little at the bonds before him. I began to ease the Lycra knickers down, inch by inch, my heart beating faster and somehow louder, in the presence of my solo audience.

Once my panties were removed, I straightened up and moved my hands to my upper body, the left hand teasing the skin at the top of my cleavage, the right toying with the zip that secured my snug-fitting camisole.

Lee stared raptly at the fingers that caressed the zip. Again I moved slowly, making a great show of playing with the clasp, before finally beginning to slide it down the length of the bodice in time to a long drawn-out sigh from my confined companion.

Standing naked, the warm air of the room soft against the slightly sticky sheen of my breasts, I too let out the briefest of sighs, a fact that wasn't missed by Lee, who looked at me sharply for a second, as if only just comprehending how much my control of him was turning me on. I knew then that I couldn't wait any longer.

"Come here." I barked the words, returning Lee's expression to one of confusion. "Bend over the bed. Knees on the floor."

Without the use of his arms he obeyed clumsily, dropping to the floor and leaning across the bed, crushing the thick duvet beneath his stomach. His arse stuck out perfectly, giving me excellent access as I soothed its uneven texture with both palms. Moving closer, so that the fronts of my legs pushed against the backs of his, I increased the pressure of my hands until, unable to resist any longer, I smacked his right cheek, hard.

"Fuck!" Lee's alarmed shout was muffled by the bedclothes.

He tried to stand, but I'd preempted the move, and held the flat of his back still with all the strength my free hand could muster as I hit him again.

He continued to swear as the strikes built up, but made no further attempt to escape his punishment. Reassured that Lee wasn't going to try and pull away, I added my left hand to the fray, and built up a steady rhythm of slaps across his arsecheeks, creating an attractive pattern of growing pinkish-red blotches against the contrasting pale skin. Lee's stream of obscenities subsided into throaty whimpers. It was the sign I'd been waiting for, and stopping my assault, I leaned forward to kiss the flesh I had so enjoyed damaging, changing his whimpers into a long moan of desire.

Turning my kisses into loitering licks across his butt, I savored the taste and aroma of Lee's heated flesh, feeling him give the occasional involuntary quiver beneath my ministrations. I drew back then, but unable to leave my prize completely, I pressed my right index finger against the top of his crack. Every muscle in Lee tightened as I left my finger in place; saying nothing, doing nothing, but making him wait.

When the tension of my inaction got to be too much for me, I fished under the duvet for a tube of lube. I flipped its lid open with my free hand, and savoring the anticipation of his reaction, I replaced my poised finger with the nozzle of the tube, and squeezed.

"Shit!" Right on cue Lee gave an involuntary jerk off the bed, but again I'd been prepared, and held him in place by jamming my knees into the back of his crouched legs. "What the fuck are you doing, woman?"

Easing a digit into the clear cold gel, I began to massage it over the outer rim of his dark hole, before edging it inside. "Isn't it obvious, honey, I'm using my equipment."

"What? I don't…"

"Don't what?" I spoke softly, continuing to maneuver into his arse, taking delight in the clenching of his muscles as they puckered against my exploration. "Are you honestly telling me you are not enjoying yourself?"

"But I…" Lee's groans grew deeper as I began to delve farther.

"You've never had this done to you before. Am I right? Has no one ever buggered this beautiful backside baby? Has no one ever shown you how wonderful it feels to be fucked in this way? Are you really telling me that Lee Cooper, Mr. Sex himself, is an arse-fuck virgin?"

"I…" Lee's sentence stalled again. I glanced around at his face. Buried into the depths of my duvet, I could make out his tightly closed eyes and his crimson-flushed cheeks.

Patting his rump with my free hand, I continued, "So, this belongs to me then. This entrance is just mine. But, I'm not a cruel woman, Mr. Cooper. If you want me to stop, I'll stop. All you have to do is say the word *stop*, and I'll end this, and you can go." My finger was in up to the hilt now, and I propelled it gently, working the lube deep into him. "So, shall I stop?"

The stifled whine that came from his throat was indecipherable, and so I asked again as a second digit joined the first. "What was that, honey?"

"Please…"

"Please what?" I began to smack his arsecheeks with the small round leather paddle I'd hidden amongst my toys. "Please carry on? Please hit me harder? Please fuck me with something thicker? 'Cos I have something thicker here, honey. I have all the equipment I could possibly need."

Sweat was prickling across Lee's back as I trailed the edge of the paddle between his shoulder blades and down his spine, listening carefully, expecting him to shout out for me to stop, but still he said nothing.

I could have left my fingers within him longer, so much was I enjoying the sensation of his hole grasping at me, but my body was beginning to demand more attention, and I suddenly resented the fact that Lee's expert hands were captive, and therefore couldn't run over my tight breasts, or explore the growing throb between my legs.

"As you have not asked me to stop, then I must assume you like your current situation, and so..." I retrieved a long thick butt plug from beneath the duvet. Stretching my arm out, I waved the blue plastic length in front of his eyes, "See what I have here? I'm sure it'll be a perfect fit."

Lee's eyes opened, and blinked, but he said nothing.

"Do you want me to pop this in, babe? You'll have to ask me nicely." My pussy twitched as I waited to hear him beg. Surely I had done enough to make him want it.

"I..." Again he said no more, so I increased the momentum, and slipped a hand between his legs, trailing a finger along the length of his dick. The growl that left his lips was deep and gruff as I maneuvered my hand farther between him and the bedcovers, brushing his tip with the lightest of touches.

"Was that a *please* I heard then?"

"Oh, shit, oh, fuck."

"Swearing at me will simply make me want to punish you more, honey." And to prove my point, I hit him swiftly with my palm, leaving both my hand and his buttocks stinging.

"Do it, please, do it!" Lee's voice cracked with need as he blurted out his request.

"Do what, honey?"

"Fuck my arse. Stick that thing in me. Please!!"

My sigh of victory came out in strangled relief as I removed my fingers and replaced them with the butt plug, relishing the quiet low whimpers that escaped from his throat as Lee's muscles were stretched to capacity.

With the plug in place, its cap suctioning against his arse, I instructed him to shuffle up the bed and turn over. Untying his wrists, I lay on top of him, and staring into his watering, hungry eyes, I eased his cock between my slick pussy lips. "So honey, do I have the equipment?"

Lee lifted his stiff arms to my tits, and began to knead them with wonderfully rough pinches. I plunged against him, my head full of the fact that he was being fucked from both sides. Grunting out his words, the mechanic brought his lips to my neck, nipping with savage bites. "I think you could say that."

Abandoning my mistress pose in the face of my curiosity, I asked, "How does it feel, babe?"

"As firsts go, this is one of the best." Lee bought his arms around to my backside and began to spank me in retaliation for my treatment of him. Then, without warning, he slid a finger into my anus, and I moaned in ecstasy as his mouth crushed mine.

It was too much for me, already close to overload from my conquest of his virgin backside; I felt the tension climb within my stomach just as Lee grabbed my pigtail and yanked it sharply. As he closed his eyes into tight lines, spots of red dotted across my lover's chest as we thrust harder against each other. Every nerve in my body seemed to ignite at once, and suddenly we were both coming in an outpouring of mutual groans.

Lee's hands ran through the pile of sex toys that remained hidden beneath my duvet, his fingers lingering over the silk tie I'd so recently restrained him with.

Standing next to me, he picked up a second, thicker, butt plug. "I'd never seen one of these in real life before." He looked at me out of the corner of his eye. "Do you like using it on yourself?"

I smiled mischievously. "Yes, I do." I nodded in the direction of the toy he held so reverently. "That one is not for beginners, honey."

"You play with all of this stuff on your own?" He weighed a frighteningly long vibrator in his palm as he spoke.

"Most of it." I could feel the heat of the room rise around us as I replied, "For some things, I need a friend."

"Well, then." Lee stood up straighter, his voice returning to its usual sexy confidence. Putting a strong hand on my shoulder, he steered me bodily around, so that I was facing my armchair. "I think you'd better bend over that chair, young lady. After all, you have been a very, very naughty girl, and right now, I seem to be in control of all your equipment...."

STILL LIFE

Sommer Marsden

He only does it because I need it. Because I ask for it. And we only do it twice a year, maybe three.

"Stand back there, Marilee," Jess says and then takes measured steps back to where we started, the lone double bed spread with snowy white sheets surrounded by what seems like acres and acres of mannequins.

I strike a pose and try not to hope. Or daydream. My long black hair runs in ribbons down my pale skin. One nipple peeks through. I'm cold and excited. All the years of modeling, covers and mannequin work, parties and raves. I am most at home here among plasticine sisters while Jess gives me what I crave.

He leaves me, but only for a while. You would think that I would break my pose while I wait. Lie on the bed, sit on the floor. Find a chair for Christ's sake. You would be wrong.

"So, you're like...an artist?" Her voice is high and she's popping her gum, something that drives me insane, and Jess knows it. That is his little joke. His little fuck-you to me for asking this of him. It's me who likes the women. Not Jess.

"I am like an artist. Come on in." His voice, properly fluid, dark and warm, makes my skin shiver. The sound of him. The sound of their feet on the steps and the girl's high tinkly laugh.

"Wow. This is kind of creepy. And cool," she says. *Pop, pop, pop* goes the wad in her mouth. Even from back here—back in the cheap seats, so to speak—I can see the pink flash of bubble gum on her tongue. Her eyes track the sea of bodies: naked tits, plastic crotches; some dressed in black panties, some in white, some in none. I can fake fake tits. I cannot fake a hairless, seamless pussy made of plastic. So we had added panties here and there for flavor and camouflage.

She plops on the bed, drops her purse, peels off her jean jacket studded with broaches and buttons and baubles. "So…"

Jess stares right at me, his eyes zeroing in without hesitation and I have to remind myself to breathe the shallowest of breaths. To keep my face a mask of nothingness. A blank slate. A wordless page. He smiles. "So, what?"

"You wanna…" She twirls a streamer of bleach-blonde hair around her finger. The fingernail is painted blue and the polish is chipped. This is her version of coy.

"Fuck you?" Jess's eyes shoot to me, to her, to me again. Goose bumps roll over my naked skin and I steady my face. I cannot steady goose bumps. Even I cannot do that. No matter how good I am at being plastic.

"Well, yeah?" She shrugs, laughs, and though he has not answered she is peeling off her small tee, hot pink like her gum, her lipstick. Her bra is hot pink, too. Shocking.

Jess pops one of her breasts out before she gets the bra off. He rolls his thumb over her rosy nipple and she purrs like a cat. "You like that?" She nods. My pussy grows wet under my black panties. I watch him touch this flesh and blood, nonperfect, gum-chewing girl. And I want him to fuck her. And then me. Maybe then I will feel real again.

Jess tells me I am quite real. That I am just like everyone else. I try. But I feel more like the women who surround me, the ones that were manufactured. Bald, painted, poseable. Fake.

Jess watches me, dark brown eyes burning my skin and torching my fast-beating heart. He frowns for a moment. I know what he wants. He wants me to walk forward, stop him, call it off. He wants me not to want this. And he wants me to feel right. And he loves me. Since he loves me, he gives me this. And he hates it. Do you see how vicious that fucking little circle of craziness is? It hurts your head, doesn't it? I know it hurts mine.

I stay still, as impossibly still and flawless as the five-foot-ten molded plastic woman next to me. A still life. A work of art. Perfect.

I don't say a word. So Jess climbs on. Another club girl. Another conquest. I like to watch him with them because when I am jealous my heart beats faster, my pussy gets wetter, my thoughts gets louder. I am more real. "You like that, Amy?" he says her name. He says it so I will know that her name is Amy and yes, he will fuck her if I don't stop him.

I watch.

His mouth on her mouth. He's taken her gum. His mouth on her throat, her nipple, biting the inside of her breast in the way that always makes my throat feel too small and my cunt beat like another heart. He pins her tiny hands above her head on the white, white bed. She's making little noises like she's crying, but when she turns her head, I see the smile there. Jess is licking his way down her. Down her torso, over the swell of her little belly (I have none). He pushes his face between her legs and I close my eyes, breaking from my stillness for a moment, because I know how good his tongue feels on my clit. Broad and warm and wet.

I know the exact pressure he uses to lick and the force he uses to suck and I know that once I come he likes to still keep going, likes to keep licking and sucking because, he says, that is when I taste the sweetest—like raw sugar or clover honey.

"Oh, god," she says. *Amy* says. She says *Oh, god,* as if she has invented it. But I don't blame her, because when I open my eyes I can see the tip of Jess's tongue riding the tiny cleft of her pussy. And I know that what she is saying is all she can think to say.

Her hands, one stamped with the club logo, shove into his long brown hair and she touches him the way I want to. She runs her fingers over his face like a blind woman and she arches her hips up, hooks one leg (shorter than mine) around his shoulder and thrusts up so he can eat her more: harder, faster, wetter…more.

His eyes find me again. He knows just where I am even in this sea of look-alikes. It stops my heart, that look, but I do not respond. Then he's over her, the petite bleach-blonde Amy and he's tracing her hot pink lips with his dick. The blunt rosy head of his cock brushes her lip like he's applying her lipstick and her tongue darts out to taste him. I feel a rush of fluid slide from my pussy but I do not break my stance. That would be unacceptable. This is about them, right now. Not me.

"Suck my dick, Amy. Suck it like a good girl. Put your little pink tongue on me, girl." He's saying it for me but she's eating it up. Amy likes the dirty talk.

"Yes, Jess," she says and laughs. I know she is laughing because it rhymes. Because that's the kind of girl she is. But then he's fucking her mouth, long even, hard strokes but his eyes are on me. I feel sweat prickle my upper lip. My heart jumps so hard it hurts. My body hums with jealousy and wanting him. I watch the muscles in his stomach flex as he shoves his cock deep into her little pink throat.

She's lapping at him. Sucking. Making noises. Wet noises, happy noises, porn-movie noises as she takes every thrust he gives. Jess is white knuckling it, holding the stunted headboard of the prop bed in his studio like a drowning man holding tight to a piece of driftwood. I can read his mind. If he comes now, he will only have had oral with this strange girl. He will not have really cheated on me all the way at least. It won't be real if it's just a blowjob and a tawdry few minutes of going down on Bubble Gum Barbie. I stare at him, willing him to do what I've asked.

He does.

Jess pulls free of her mouth, his face set and angry almost. Not at her. At me. The first time I told him I wanted to see him with real girls, he damn near left me. *You are a real girl!* He had yelled and shouted and raged. It took everything I had to tell him: *No. No I'm not. At least I do not feel I am.*

He called me crazy. But he did it.

"Spread your legs," he says to her. The muscles in my shoulder lock up and a spasm takes root in my pinky. I could shift my stance and she would never know right now because Jess is spearing her angrily with his perfect hard-on. But I do not move a muscle. His eyes lock with hers and he thrusts high and then higher still. The bleach-blonde top of her head bangs the headboard. She hooks a long, bottle-tanned leg around his waist and arches up to meet him.

"Fuck me, Daddy," she says in her little-girl voice. "Fuck me hard, Daddy."

My cunt tightens, a spasm works through me and I clench the floor of my pelvic muscles. A fine cold sweat pops up on my upper lips. "Cunt," Jess says and she laughs. "Filthy little whore."

"Yes," says the blonde. "I like it dirty, Daddy."

I hate her. And at that moment, I hate him. But most of all I hate me because my pussy is beating with a heart of its own and I'm watching his fingers brush her very real skin. A bruise here, a scar there, blonde hair on her arms shining in the bright loft overheads. She is not perfect and airbrushed and flawless. She has stubble on her legs and she chews like a cow.

"Whore!" Jess says and his eyes lock with mine. I break my stance for just a heartbeat to lick my lips. I'd give every spread I'd ever done in every magazine ever printed to kiss him right now. He grins, pulls from her and crawls down her marked-up, imperfect body like he has a score to settle.

Deep down, he probably does.

Jess kicks the bedsheets from around him, and they catch for a moment on his long, muscular leg. He buries his face between her thighs. I can see beautiful silver stretch marks from here. He licks in long pink curls up between her outer lips, working his tongue so she pants like a dog. He pinches her pert little clit between his white, white teeth and smiles at me, the tiny pebble of flesh captured there so I can see. He smiles and buries his face again. His nose disappears and she arches up, clawing at his hair, coming like some porn queen.

"Yes, baby, yes!" she crows and her knees, pudgier than mine, clamp around Jess's beloved head as she comes again, his fingers buried in her cunt, his nose hidden in her flesh.

Then he returns to stabbing her with his cock, fulfilling my wish and punishing me all in one act. I watch her, perfect in her imperfection: the small roll of flesh around her middle, the mole on her hip, the cellulite on her ass. Each time he drives into her, her body rolls like a wave. I barely move, so thin and tight and perfect. Like a molded plastic girl.

I love you he tells me every time. *I love you and the way you are. You are very real to me, Marilee.*

But in that equation he is not as important as I am. He twines his finger through hers the way he does mine. And that makes me sad. The sadness is exquisite. The sadness is tangible. The sadness makes me feel alive. "Yes," I say and only I can hear it. He kisses below her jaw, bites her throat, dips his head to capture her nipple while his hips slam against her hips and she moans like she's dying. "I'm coming, Daddy," she says and Jess's eyes flick to mine like a brooding storm rushing a horizon.

I nod. Barely. I am so stiff now from not moving. Pain sparkles in my body like magic. Jess closes his eyes, bites his lip. For all the world, he looks to be concentrating. Trying to picture me he always says. Me under him, my pussy locked around him. Because he loves me. He loves me more than I ever could love me.

He comes. And my heart triple skips and hurts so bad I fear it's breaking.

Amy gets the bum's rush. She doesn't seem surprised at all. Jess escorts her down to the thumping club below his loft. I hear him in the hall. *Yeah, baby, I'll call you. I have some stuff going on. I'll give you a ring, though.* He never will. I can hear it in her voice when she agrees, that she is aware it's bullshit.

I move on numb legs to the bed, push the sheets into a messy jumble that is casual in appearance but pleasant to look at. Like a magazine illustration. Like a photo shoot. I sink down onto the still-warm bed and play my long legs over the wrinkled, damp sheets. I arrange my hair and my arms so that I am beautiful. But not too beautiful.

I try to remember the ugly face that Amy made when she came. She was a piece of writhing art locked in her orgasm, something like a painting of demons and Hell, her face contorted and imperfect in blessed agony. I make that face. It does not feel right on my face.

"Baby," Jess says. He's right there, watching me, frowning. In that one word is love and hate and worry.

"Baby, no more."

I hold my arms out. I study them like they're not mine. Long and pale and thin. Too thin in real life but on glossy expensive paper they are the arms of a goddess. An angel. He comes to me. He smells like fucking and bubble gum. I kiss him, suck his tongue. Taste her. A sugary rush with an acrid undertone. I spread my legs and his cock, hard already in his jeans, nudges the split of my pussy. I'm so wet. So ready. Waiting to feel.

He's dirty and covered in her. He's flawless.

I let him look at me for three heartbeats. Me, a still life, a painting. And then I say, "Shh," and kiss him. Push up at him with my hips. Press my pelvis to his. Beg him with my body not to talk or question or analyze but just to fuck me. Take me. Right here in the bed that smells like her.

I push at his jeans. Tug at his cock. Free him and slide the hard ridge of him to my hot, hot pussy. I open for him, crying. When I cry I am ugly. I am real.

Jess stares, licks off my tears and drives into me. His teeth capture my earlobe and he bites. I cry harder, coming so fast, so soon. His lips lick over mine, trailing the cloying taste of bubble gum with each slippery swipe. "I love you," he says.

I cry harder. I clench my cunt around him, pulling at his lower back, desperate, needy, entirely unattractive but swelling with emotion. I feel so much I must be gorgeous.

"I love you." He stares at me, moving slower. Fucking me with his eyes and his cock. "Say you love me, Marilee."

"I love you." I mean it, but it's hard.

"Say you love *you*, Marilee." This time he traps my cheeks in his hands.

I shake my head, another orgasm rushing at me like a purple

white wave. My vision goes bright, my cunt gushes and crushes around him. He moves faster, his eyes dark and dangerous and full of hope.

I shake my head. He pinches me. "Say it, Marilee."

"I love me," I say, sobbing. And I come. I come and my face is ugly and his face is perfect and for one split second, I am as real as bubble gum and stretch marks and extra flesh. For one heartbeat I am perfectly real.

SECRET SERVICE

Rachel Kramer Bussel

Some people go to culinary school with dreams of becoming the next Michelin-starred chef and reviving American cuisine. Me, I just wanted to make people happy, namely women, and the only thing that rivals food, to my mind, is sex. My plan all along had been to combine them in the form of one-stop shopping. I couldn't exactly blurt this out while attending the Culinary Institute of America, so instead I bided my time, working as a chef in top restaurants in New York, Miami, L.A., San Francisco and Seattle, taking note of everything that was done well and everything I thought could be improved.

I perfected my cooking technique, while also bedding plenty of my fellow chefs as well as servers, busboys, hostesses and customers. Closing time took on new meaning as I kissed someone whose breath smelled of the food I'd just prepared, and that's when the idea for Secret Service was formed. I was living in Brooklyn by then and my inspiration came from Kokie's, a bar that, before it closed a few years back, did a brisk backroom business in cocaine. (Google "Kokie's Place" if you don't believe me.) You could walk in, order a beer, casually inquire about doing a bump, then get whisked away and emerge high and happy.

My friends and I had marveled at how such a business had managed to stay afloat at all, its name taunting all comers. Now you couldn't just walk in and go up to the bartender, wave a rolled-up dollar bill and be given a mirror and some blow. It was more subtle than that, and it was the very subtlety, the sly maneuvering, that gave me my brainstorm: I wanted to open the Kokie's of cunnilingus, a restaurant that would offer a little something extra in the back, geared specifically toward women who wanted a few minutes to spread their legs, lean back, and get licked and sucked by an expert mouth.

The whole thing was kind of an in joke, to some people at least. But to my employees and customers, it was a brilliant merger of supply and demand. It was like the sexual equivalent of fast food; women didn't have to wait around for what they really wanted. Sure, most of them could've found a man to take them home and fuck them, but finding one to take them home and simply focus his tongue on their most private parts, focusing solely on their pleasure? That was rarer, and I knew there were plenty of women who would rather pay for their orgasm, in addition to enjoying a fine meal. And I was right. From our opening night, we were a big hit.

I thought of it kind of like the In-N-Out secret menu; we didn't post a sign or have something on the menu saying, *Sides: French Fries: $5; Cunnilingus: $20.* That would simply be tacky. As distinctly modern as my concept was, there was something old-fashioned about how the gossip spread, and watching women emerge from the back room with that flushed sex high lighting up their faces made me glow with a satisfaction money can't buy.

Working at restaurants had given me a taste of what it meant to sell a kind of oral bliss; watch anyone dig into a truly superior meal, whether it's macaroni and cheese or tiramisu or even a plate of perfectly cooked spinach, and you will see a look that rivals orgasm on her face. By catering largely to women, I hoped to give them a space where they could enjoy the food as well as the extras in peace, without a care as to what their man, or any man, might think.

Don't get me wrong, though; word spread even before our official opening to the right kind of guy, the kind who wants to see his woman satisfied, who gets hard thinking about his woman in the throes of ecstasy. My phone was ringing off the hook with men making reservations and subtly inquiring as to how they could comp their lady of the evening a turn backstage. Business was booming and opening night was booked solid two weeks in advance. I had planned an extensive advertising campaign, but found that I didn't even need it. The ones who needed it found me.

I would have loved to install secret cameras so I could watch what really went down back there, but my ethics wouldn't allow it, and I wanted the men I hired to feel uninhibited as well. How did I choose them? Well, I didn't have any ethical qualms about putting them on the restaurant version of a casting couch. I was too busy putting my business plan into action to really date, and, like many of my customers, I wasn't interested in the whole wining and dining drama. I'd have time for that later; I wanted to cut to the chase, and while I have an extensive collection of sex toys that I make good use of, they simply can't rival the human touch required for proper cunnilingus. I've been given head by dozens of exuberant men, as well as a handful of very talented women, so I think I know what goes into pussy-eating, even though mileage may vary depending on your preferences.

I set up timers so the women would have an idea of the limitations of what they were ordering; if they wanted to continue their private pleasure outside the restaurant, they were more than welcome to. My employees were free agents, and many of them wound up rolling out at closing time right into the beds of women they'd serviced earlier in the night.

For me, the most important thing, the one element I can't live without, is for the person putting my pussy where his mouth to want to be there, not just for the money or for what comes afterward, but because that's what makes him horny. It's true what they say: good eaters are good at going down; picky eaters rarely make good lovers. I trained my associates, making sure they were comfortable with the job. There'd be plenty of downtime, since I couldn't exactly ask my customers to make appointments for when they wanted their happy endings, so my staff might have to go down on several women in a row. "Could you handle it?" I'd grill potential pussy-eaters during interviews as I fed them my special calamari or my roast duck. A free meal or two was part of the interview process. I'd listen closely to their answers, trying to get at the heart of why they wanted a job that essentially boiled down to being a tongue for hire.

The men whose demeanors changed as they discussed the pleasures of giving head were the ones who got a callback. I could hear something in their voices, a tone that got more hushed, an unmistakable reverence as they sang the praises of pussy as intensely as they did the flavor of an imported olive oil. They were true sensualists, and while their job wouldn't take place in the kitchen, I wanted them to appreciate both kinds of services my business would provide. Similarly, my chefs had to know about the importance of the taste buds to arousal, the connection between the two sets of lips. I wanted the joys my customers experienced, whether the fiery spice of a chili or a mouth sucking hard on their clit, the thrillingly sweet smooth-ness of the perfect gelato or a tongue caressing their innermost parts, to match, to complement one another. I'll admit, too, that I found my own sex pulsing with desire as those I interviewed talked. I employed a few women as well, in the kitchen and in back, because I wanted to appeal to as wide a range of customers as possible, and sometimes what a woman needs most is another woman to set her at ease and then shake her world so intensely she sees stars.

I liked the play on words that "Secret Service" conveyed, as well as the hiding in plain sight nature of the name, just like Kokie's before it. I secured my staff, and brought my friends in over the next two months for trial runs. They were more than happy to subject themselves to meal after exquisite meal, not to mention providing feedback on the oral offerings. I quickly realized we'd need to play our music on the louder side to cover up the women's screams of arousal; one room was an actual closet, soundproofed, for the real screamers. What I heard from my friends let me know right away that we had something big on our hands. My phone started ringing off the hook, my inbox exploding with requests for reservations from people who'd heard through the grapevine about what was really on the menu at my restaurant—or rather, off the menu. Except that in this case, I hadn't waited for my customers to request an amorous appetizer, I'd anticipated their needs before they had.

Tara, the publicist I hired, was instructed to not speak openly about anything other than the food, but she perfected the art of the double entendre. Having taken her own personal tour of every head-giver on staff, she knew whereof she spoke when she peppered her press release with words like "satisfaction," "orgasmic," "completely unique," and "female-oriented." Even so, the average reader wouldn't have a clue unless they heard from someone what (and who) was really going down. Opening night, I fluttered around nervously, hoping that advance buzz, curiosity and general horniness would all work in our favor.

Reporters swarmed the place, and I knew from careful observation that more than one female restaurant critic had made her way to the back while waiting for her meal to be served, later tucking into her order with the gusto of the freshly tongue-fucked.

But I was more curious about what the average woman thought. If there had been an ethical way to set up a camera to peek in at the booths in the back, I'd have done so. I was busy overseeing the cooks, making sure people were seated quickly, trying to look like I wasn't frantic. I must have failed miserably because Ed, my second in charge, pulled me aside. "Kate, you're making people nervous. You have to stop pacing. Come with me." He tugged me into one of the back rooms that happened to be empty. "You know what you need. This whole place is simply your fantasy writ large. Now keep quiet and sit back and relax."

He shoved me into a chair while I spluttered, my mouth open. "Not now. Later, after everyone leaves. I can't let you do this right now."

"Why not, exactly?" he asked, snaking his hand up my jean skirt and slipping his fingers into my waistband. I was wet against his touch even as I heard what could only be the sounds of a woman in the throes of orgasm from the other side of the wall.

I bit my lower lip, worrying it with my teeth as no good answer came to mind. There was little I could do at that point, anyway, and now that he'd gotten me so riled up, I feared I wouldn't be able to relax if I didn't get off immediately. "Plus I bet you're dying to know what I can do with my mouth." He was on to me; I'd hired him in part for his impressive resume, but also because he had a goatee, big hands, and tattoos that made me want to tackle him and strip him naked. Now he was about to do the same to me, and I was about to let him.

I shut my eyes as he shoved my skirt up and then took a Swiss army knife out of his pocket and sliced right through my wet white panties, balling them up and shoving them in his jeans pocket. The click of the knife echoed in the air, but he kept it in his hand as he held on to my skirt and then placed his mouth against my lips. I'd expected him to dive right in, but he started slow, breathing in my scent, rubbing his lips gently against mine before allowing his tongue to make contact. "Relax," he whispered, making me realize that I hadn't fully done so. I let my arms go slack, my fingers tight against the chair's back, and rested my heels against Ed's shoulder blades as he showed me that he could've just as easily applied for a job on his knees, rather than in the office.

While in the rest of his life he's a blur of energy, as he licked me, he took his time, giving me slow lap after slow lap of his warm tongue. Then he started fluttering it, fast little flicks that made my nostrils flare as I bucked upward against him. He pushed my hips down, and I struggled to get closer. "Next time I do this, I'm going to have to tie you up," he said, and I melted back down, both at the idea that there'd be a next time and the image of me bound with black rope, unable to move.

His tongue pressed inside me, filling my hole as best he could, even as my hard clit silently begged to be touched, sucked, kissed. Slowly, every thought about the future of the restaurant, all the stress of the past few months that had culminated on this monumental day, disappeared into his mouth, replaced simply by the need to come. That need was one I welcomed, one I treasured, for even though I'd made time for sessions with my vibrator, even sneaking a quiet one into my office for a few minutes of stolen pleasure, it wasn't the same as a man whose mission was to make me climax. Everything about Ed's actions told me he was as into it as I was, that his enjoyment fed directly from mine. He hummed against my sex, not as part of some new-age sex tip he'd read, but to express himself, half hum, half "Mmm," as he coaxed forth more and more of my juices.

He lifted his head at the critical juncture, making me jerk mine upward. "Don't stop," I panted.

"I wouldn't dream of it, Kate," he said, then gave me the lightest kiss, a peck, really, but one that let me taste my own saltiness on his lips. His thick thumb pressed inside me, curving down toward my ass, then swiveling up to press toward my G-spot. Soon the thumb was gone, replaced by other fingers, several of them, while his palm pressed on my lower belly. He curved his fingers just so and I bit my lip even harder, rocking my head up and down since clearly moving my hips wasn't permitted in our silent little power play.

His fingers twisted inside me just as my muscles clamped down, a sensual tug of war that ended when he pressed four fingers into me, stretching my poor cunt, opening me up as he sank down once again to devote his lips to my clit. In concert, his fingers and mouth serviced me, summoned me, scattered my senses all over the room as they delivered their two-pronged attack. My clit met his teeth, a feral greeting befitting my now-frantic state. His teeth held my bud steady as his tongue speared it, and his fingers seemed to grow inside me, though I knew that wasn't technically possible. He made me feel so big, my pussy becoming a powerful giant capable of ruling the entire world, even as he narrowed it to this singular sensation. When my climax finally roared from within me, I felt its power leap out from the mouth of my pussy like dragon's breath, fierce and dangerous, a five-alarm fire that clanged its way from my center outward. He stayed glued to me but gradually stilled, his fingers slackening, his tongue pausing, as he gave us both time to recover.

Eventually he pulled out, licked his fingers, then scooped me up in his arms, arranging me into a standing position and pulling my skirt down. "You've done good, Kate," he whispered in my ear, and I wasn't sure if he meant with coming or the opening. "And just so you know, if you're ever short a man back here, you can count on me."

The rest of the night passed in a blur, at least for me, a happy one as I floated around helping out as needed, urging women who seemed reluctant to take even just a quick moustache ride in back. "It's on me," I told a few of them, sensing that this was the kind of freebie that would ensure some truly dedicated customers.

The looks they gave me were priceless—before and after. So many versions of the raised eyebrow, the quizzical glance, the knowing grin. Some women were clearly unsure of what they were getting into, but the true New Yorkers, the gutsy types, were willing to boldly go where their friends could only ogle.

The next day, the papers were abuzz about the outstanding service, the off-the-menu specialties, the attention to detail. Even the food got high praise and the phone rang off the hook for the next month, ensuring a full house every night. I couldn't get Ed off my mind, and invited him back to my place after work one night to see what he could do in a more relaxed atmosphere. If I'd thought ten minutes with him was heavenly, try three hours. I was literally weak in the knees when he was done. It hadn't been a fluke; he was magically able to get me to relax, then get me to come, or keep me on the edge. His mouth made love to me in the most incredible of ways, without his trying to show off or be macho, and certainly without a hint of asking for anything in return. Eventually, though, after I'd begged, he'd showed me the present hiding in his pants. My nostrils flared as I sucked in a deep breath at the sight. It was so tempting, but he told me he'd rather we kept our arrangement focused on me. "But...you like it, right? Eating pussy turns you on? This isn't just some job for you, is it?" I was horrified at the thought.

"Of course not," he said, stroking my hair the way I longed to stroke his cock. "I'm not saying I'll never fuck you, but for now, I want this to be about you. I want you to know you can trust me, with your pussy and your business. I can do it on command, or I can do it like this, with you, where it's like a feast. I have to pace myself so I don't come in my pants like a teenager. I'm getting to know what you like, where you want to be touched, how soft, how rough. That's enough for me for now." No man had ever said anything like that to me. We'd always been in too much of a hurry to tear our clothes off. Yes, even on long, lazy vacations. We'd bake ourselves in the sun, then swim in the water, then someone's hands would wander and we'd almost wind up fucking on a public beach. Never had I met a man with more patience than me, especially when it came to sex. I sank back and let him work his magic one more time. I forced my mind to let go of everything it wanted to think, every thought it was tempted to send wending its way through my orgasm. I floated there, even with my body firm against the bed. Ed made me float, made me rise and soar and then sink back to the sheer delight of his tongue and lips, his heat and passion. He made me feel so special that night, allowing me to relax in a way I hadn't in longer than I could remember.

Having him around has made even the most maddening moments of running a restaurant feel like no big deal. All I have to do is think about how calmly he approaches everything he does, how he always has a knowing wink, and, when need be, a lusty appetite that isn't sated until I am.

Some people have asked when I'm going to open a corresponding restaurant for men, and don't worry, I'm already working on it. It'll be called BJ's, and I can't wait to hang the COMING SOON sign on the door.

SHIFT CHANGE

Emerald

I hoisted the shoulder strap on my briefcase as I headed through the mall. When I reached the Apple store, I went straight back to the Genius Bar, aka the technical support center of the Apple world. I had an appointment and was right on time, so I hoped they wouldn't take very long. Being without my computer felt to me like being dropped in the middle of a desert island.

There were no other customers at the Genius Bar, and the GENIUS behind it, his denotation as such announced by his shirt, asked if he could help me as I pulled my MacBook Pro from my briefcase and set it between us. His name tag said JAKE, and I introduced myself and explained that my laptop wasn't getting past the gray loading screen upon startup. He nodded once, businesslike, and plugged in my computer before flipping it open and pushing the power button.

As he did so, I took a closer look at him. Upon first glance I hadn't found him particularly attractive, but as I watched him he began to seem right on the line between classic tech geek and an understated sexiness. His expression was serious as he watched the screen, its bright light reflected in the lenses of his glasses as he typed and clicked and probed and whatever else the Apple Geniuses do when someone brings in a problematic computer.

The more I watched him, the more mesmerizing he became. He wasn't the kind of guy I usually found myself attracted to, the kind that turned my head on the street and brought an unsolicited "Fuck me please" forward in my brain. He was the kind who had to be watched like this, instigator of a quieter kind of attraction that came out only when all the characteristics that showcased his sexiness—focus, intensity, knowledge— came together for display. Even when he spoke, he did so with concise, no-nonsense syllables in a tone neither dull nor distant. Everything about his professional focus and action seemed to flow, but in a very structured manner—like liquid through a straw.

And suddenly I wanted him to direct that attention at me.

A second Genius appeared behind him, also clad in the tell-tale GENIUS-labeled shirt. He looked at the screen and said, "Startup trouble?"

"Yeah. I'm checking the hard drive," Jake answered.

The second technician looked at me then and smiled. And my stomach jumped. This was the kind of guy I was usually attracted to, the cocky, roughly sexy, hot kind that I wanted to grab me by the hair and shove his cock into me hard. I noted his name tag, which stated NICK, and introduced myself. The way he looked me up and down brought heat rising up in me like lava from a volcano, as I was already simmering from my response to Jake. The Apple store was a hell of a lot more interesting that I had remembered.

Jake had continued clicking sporadically and finally looked

up at me. "The hard drive is fine, which is good, but it's either a memory problem or the operating system is defunct. It might require a reinstallation, which will mean I'll need to back everything up onto another hard drive first."

I nodded, attempting to look like I had a clue what he was talking about. "Right."

He smiled then. And what a delightful smile he had. It was the first time he had done so, and I smiled back, sheepishly, and shrugged.

"Okay, so I have no idea what you're talking about. But I'm assuming you do."

He chuckled and reached down to pull out a contraption of some sort and a power cord, hooking it all up with the same efficiency with which he had done everything since I had started observing him.

Someone sidled up and leaned against the other end of the Genus Bar. "How's it going?" he asked the two behind it. "Busy?"

"Not really," Nick answered. He nodded my direction. "Stacey here has just brought us her non-starting-up MacBook Pro, which Jake has been working diligently on." His flirtatious sarcasm fit precisely with the cocky impression I had of him so far—as well as with the image I still had of him holding me down and slamming his cock into me. I smirked and turned to the new arrival.

"Hello, Stacey. I'm Andrew," he said, offering his hand.

I shook it and batted my eyelashes as bait. "You appear to be a Genius too," I said, indicating his shirt. He had an outgoing attractiveness about him, and I was starting to feel like I should come apply for a job in some capacity at the Apple store.

"Yeah. I'm not on the clock yet though," Andrew said. "I just got here. I don't start for another twenty minutes." He sent me a lazy grin. "So you'll have to get by with these two until then. If they haven't got it figured out by five, I'll take care of it for you."

"It's under control." Jake made his first contribution to the conversation, his eyes not leaving the screen.

"Well, I guess I'll just sit here and talk to you until it's time for me to go to work," Andrew said with a wink, hoisting himself onto the stool next to me.

I beamed internally, glancing at the two behind the bar working on my laptop, the glowing little apple winking back at me as if to take a sly kind of credit for leading me to this position.

"So is one of you getting ready to leave when Andrew starts?" I asked Jake and Nick.

"Yeah," Nick answered. "I'll be out of here soon."

Jake was mostly ignoring us as he pulled a CD from a drawer beneath him and blew on it before inserting it into my machine. I bit my lip; it was an incredibly sexy gesture coming from him.

"And what about you? Are you almost done or just got here or midshift?"

Jake glanced up. "I'm here until closing. I'm actually going to go out back for my break when I'm done with this," he added to Andrew.

"Out back?" I couldn't help asking.

"The alley out the back door. It's where Nick and I go for our smoke breaks and Jake goes to get away from people," Andrew laughed. "We seem to be the only ones who ever go out there."

I nodded. I saw the idea immediately as it formed in my head, and I almost laughed at my own predictability.

"It does seem appropriate for you to take a break," I said to Jake, "having been so focused on my computer. Which I appreciate. I imagine you must be ready to toss it out the window about now."

Jake smiled as he moved his fingers over the track pad, his eyes on the screen. "It's my job."

"Your place out back sounds intriguing," I continued. "I guess at least one of you has to be here all the time though, which dashes my idea of a little impromptu gangbang there."

Nick and Jake looked up at me in unison. It was the most I had seen Jake's attention pulled from my computer since I had come in. I smiled, and Nick guffawed. All three relaxed as they interpreted my comment as a joke.

My lighthearted smile had been orchestrated for that result— I was just testing the environment. It seemed to me that while they thought I had been joking, it had caught their interest. I determined there was enough of it there for me to proceed. I hoped so anyway.

I laughed with them. "So you're about to go on break, Jake, Nick's about to get off work, and you haven't started yet," I said, turning to Andrew.

Andrew looked at me. I could tell he was wondering what I was getting at, and I decided to eliminate all suspense. I met his eyes.

"So if I went out back and stood against the wall where I imagine you stand outside and smoke your cigarettes, you could all come out one at a time and fuck me."

Jake and Nick, who had both returned to my computer, missed this comment as they talked amongst themselves, my supposed comical remark forgotten for the time being. Only Andrew, who was still focused on me, looked at me in disbelief.

I gave him a sidelong glance. "Since you seem to be the only one paying attention at this point, and since you're not on the clock yet, you could go first," I suggested. "Don't worry, I have condoms in my purse. Would you be kind enough to show me to your secret outdoor hangout?"

Andrew's expression didn't change, and I felt a twinge of disappointment as I thought he might turn the offer down. Maybe he was worried about his job, or he might have been uncomfortable with the three of them sharing such information.

"You really want us to do that?" he finally asked.

"Do you think I'd sit here and ask if I didn't?" I asked with a little laugh. "It even works out well numerically—there are three of you, and there are three places I can think of in which I'd love to be penetrated."

Nick and Jake happened to be at a lull in their own conversation at that moment, and they both looked up with a start, their stares lingering this time.

"You've missed part of the conversation," I said to them. "I was just asking Andrew to show me where to meet you all out back, but I think I can figure it out. Since one of you needs to be here all the time, you'd have to come do me one at a time. I've already invited Andrew to go first. The three of you can decide which one of you gets to fuck my mouth, which one gets my pussy, and which one gets my ass. I, incidentally, will run over to the drugstore across the street and pick up lube." I smiled at my practicality even under the circumstances. I turned to Andrew. "So I'll meet you out back in about five minutes. And if you decide you're not interested," I added to the group at large, "no hard feelings."

I slipped away from the Genius Bar and out into the mall. After completing the requisite trip to the drugstore, I reentered the mall and passed by the Apple store, stealing a glance inside at the back. Jake and Nick were side by side behind it, apparently still working on my computer. Andrew was missing.

I walked to the mall exit closest to the store, which happened to not be a public one. I pushed through one of the double metal doors and let it slam behind me. The gray expanse of concrete in front of me was deserted. I turned to the left and rounded the corner a few yards away. I saw Andrew immediately, standing against the wall beside a single gray door, smoking a cigarette. He turned and saw me.

He appeared nervous, but all I felt at that point was horny. The back of the gray building was vacant except for the two of us, just as they had said.

I walked up to him, and he turned to me, never breaking eye contact as he dropped his cigarette and crushed it out with his boot. I didn't break stride until I was touching him, my lips devouring his, the smell of cigarette smoke fresh in the cold fall air. His response held no hesitation, and his arms wrapped around me, his hands roaming from my ass up to my neck through my hair. I normally hated cigarette smoke, but I loved the way he was touching me so much that at that moment it barely fazed me.

"So where are you going to fuck me?" I whispered, my voice slightly hoarse with wanting.

Andrew sucked in his breath, and I reached down and felt the hard cock beneath his zipper.

"Your pussy," he whispered.

I smiled. Somehow this choice didn't surprise me. Wishing I had worn a skirt, I quickly unfastened my jeans and pushed them down, stepping out of them and leaving my boots on. I shimmied out of my panties as well while he watched me.

"You're going to have to undo your pants too, dear," I said with a smile as Andrew stood mesmerized. He jumped a little, then gave me a self-conscious grin as he reached for his zipper.

His cock sprang out, and I rolled the condom I had extracted from my purse down onto it. Then I backed up at the same time he moved toward me, and our bodies came together just as my back hit the concrete wall. Raising one leg, I pressed my knee into his hip, and he grabbed the back of my thigh and entered me with a thrust.

My head went back against the rough stone behind me, and I bit my lip to keep from screaming. I could feel the wetness on my thighs as he pumped into me, breathing heavily and not speaking. I met his eyes, still suppressing the moans wanting to break from my throat, as he pushed his cock into me over and over, his pace increasing with his breath as he got closer to orgasm. Finally I could take it no more and pushed my face into his shoulder, letting my scream out to be muffled by his flesh. His breathing got harsh as he came into me, pumping with abandon as his body jerked and his hand gripped the flesh of my shoulder.

He pulled out and stared at me, appearing at a loss for words.

"Thank you," I said, giving him a wink.

He smiled, and I smiled back. He moved forward to kiss me quickly, then backed away, lifting his hand in a small wave as he disappeared through the gray metal door. By the time it closed heavily behind him I was pressing my clit, making myself come within seconds of his exit. I was still breathing heavily when the door scraped open again and Jake stepped out, smiling faintly as he met my eyes.

"You look like you're ready to go," he said as he stood before me. He seemed just the way he had while working on my computer—straightforward, focused, businesslike. Even under the present circumstances the polish still seemed to be there.

It made me just as hot as I had thought it would.

I chuckled breathlessly and found that I was too aroused and out of breath to even formulate words. Jake's focused expression took on a lustful tenor as he reached down and unbuckled his belt. His focused look was on me as he undid his pants and pulled his cock out. Without instruction, I knew what part of me he had chosen to penetrate.

I smiled and gave him a wink as I dropped to my knees, taking his cock in my mouth and looking up at him as he drew in a quick breath. Knowing I only had a few minutes, I sucked hard and fast, taking his cock all the way in, growing wetter myself with every pump. Momentarily I drew back, saliva joining my lips and his cock as I looked up at him.

"I like this a little rough," I whispered. "So if you have no objections, I would be delighted if you would grab my hair and push my head onto your cock when you come."

Jake's cool demeanor almost slipped as his mouth opened slightly and his eyes half closed. I resumed sucking his dick, and he snaked a hand around to the back of my neck. He grunted quietly as he acquiesced, gripping my hair with both hands and shoving my head forward rhythmically as his hot come started to spurt into my mouth. I looked up at him and gripped the base of his cock, stroking as he finished coming, letting it run down my chin and across my lips.

When he was done, I smiled. He did too, coolly, and backed up as he tucked his cock back into his pants.

"Thank you," he said, reaching down to help me to my feet. He met my eyes. "You suck one hell of a cock." For the first time, his voice was rough, and I thought I might come at the sound. With a nod, he turned toward the door. "See you inside."

I smiled, still breathless with arousal—which was good, since I was about to get my ass fucked. I pulled a tissue out of my purse to clean the come off my face, then reached down for the bag from the drugstore and pulled out the bottle of lube.

Nick emerged from the door moments later.

"Hi," he said. "Your computer's almost ready."

I nearly laughed as I realized I had almost forgotten about my computer—the reason I was here.

Nick stepped toward me. Rather than the understated confidence and professionalism of Jake or the charming, slightly nervous appreciation of Andrew, Nick exuded more of a cockiness, the kind that usually made me salivate.

The present circumstances seemed no exception.

"So my understanding is that I get to fuck your ass," he said.

"That's right." I held up the bottle of lube.

"Well, I certainly appreciate that," Nick said, moving closer to me. He looked down at me as he said, "I haven't fucked anyone's ass for a long time. I sure didn't think I'd get the chance when I came to work today."

"Well, what a lovely coincidence." During this exchange I had pulled another condom from my purse and torn it open, and he had already freed his cock from his jeans. I looked down and slid the condom on, then glanced back up at him before turning around and bending over, planting my palms against the rough gray surface of the wall.

Nick made an approving noise as I felt him move closer to me. I heard the bottle of lube flip open, and then I felt Nick's cock nudging between my asscheeks, stopping before he penetrated me.

"I don't know how used to this you are, so I'll take my cues from you," he said. His voice was tight with arousal. I nodded and backed up slowly, pushing myself around the head of his cock and inching my way back against him until he was all the way inside my ass. I let out a breath, arching my back as the sensation and just the pure dirtiness of what we were doing shot straight to the pit of my stomach.

I could tell by Nick's breathing that he was experiencing something similar. I moved slowly back toward the wall, then back up against him, sliding his cock in and out of my ass slowly as I set the pace. When I was ready, I turned my head.

"Okay," I whispered. "You can go ahead now."

Nick pushed into me firmly, though keeping the pace not much faster than I had set it. He moaned quietly, reaching down once to slap my ass as he took it from behind. I gasped with pleasure and met his strokes, pushing back against him until I heard him grunt through clenched teeth and I knew he was coming. He gripped my hips, and I felt the wetness again between my thighs as he climaxed into me.

Nick surprised me then by reaching around in front of me with his right hand and finding my clit, stroking me there delicately as he pulled out of my ass and held me in place by my hip. I moaned, unable to keep quiet as he made me come, smacking my ass once again as he pressed firmly against my clit with his fingers.

I turned with a surprised smile. "Thank you."

He grinned. "Oh, thank you." He winked at me as he refastened his pants, then watched as I gathered my jeans and panties.

"You can go ahead," I told him. "I'll be right in."

I pulled my clothes on quickly and walked back around the corner, entering the mall through the door from which I had exited. I stopped at the restroom to do some cleanup, then headed back to the Apple store. I walked in and went straight back to the Genius Bar, where Jake and Andrew now stood huddled over my laptop. Nick was off to the side, presumably preparing to depart.

Andrew saw me first and smiled shyly. Jake looked up then as well, his penetrating gaze resting on mine.

"How's it going?" I asked casually, nodding at the laptop in front of them.

"We're running a test on it now, and that should take care of it. Should be done in just a second," Jake said.

"Don't let that stop you from coming back to see us anytime there's anything we can do for you though," Nick said from my left with a grin.

My chuckle was a little breathless. I wasn't sure how I would be handling the temptation to do exactly that as I accepted my laptop from Jake and slipped it back into my briefcase. I thanked the three of them and felt them watching me as I turned and wound among the computer-laden counters and bustling customers toward the exit.

As I approached it, I smiled as I recalled the direness I had felt about being without my computer upon entering the store an hour before. Forty-five minutes of tension relief later, I found myself wondering what might next go wrong with the computer I carried at my side. Amazing what those Geniuses can do.

ABOUT THE AUTHORS

RACHEL KRAMER BUSSEL's (rachelkramerbussel.com) books include *Bottoms Up, Spanked, Do Not Disturb, The Mile High Club, Rubber Sex, Tasting Him, Tasting Her* and *Best Sex Writing 2008, 2009* and *2010*. She's senior editor at *Penthouse Variations*, a former *Village Voice* sex columnist, and host of In the Flesh Reading Series.

When she's not plumbing the depths of kink, **CARRIE CANNON** focuses on nursing elderly houses back to health and keeping things hot in the kitchen. She's been paid to be a cookbook editor, cook, restaurant owner and a dog groomer—but writing smut is her favorite job so far.

ANGELA CAPERTON's (angelacaperton.com) fantasy novel *Woman of the Mountain* won the 2008 Eppie Award for Best Erotica. She has also published stories in several erotic anthologies including *Girls on Top, Love at First Bite, Coming Together: Against the Odds, Coming Together: Al Fresco* and *Maiden Mother Crone*.

HEIDI CHAMPA (heidichampa.blogspot.com) has appeared in more than ten anthologies including *Tasting Him, Frenzy* and *Girl Fun One*. She's also steamed up the pages of *Bust* magazine. Find her online at Clean Sheets, Ravenous Romance, Oysters and Chocolate and the Erotic Woman.

EMERALD's (thegreenlightdistrict.org) erotic fiction has been published or is forthcoming in many anthologies online and in print. She resides in suburban Maryland where she works as a webcam model and serves as an activist for reproductive freedom and sex workers' rights.

AMIE M. EVANS authors the "Two Girls Kissing" column, and is an editor, workshop provider and a retired burlesque/high-femme drag performer. On the board for Saints and Sinners LGBTQ lit fest, she graduated magna cum laude with a BA in literature and is working on her MLA at Harvard, and a novel.

SCARLETT FRENCH is a short-story writer and a poet living in London's East End with her partner, their nipper, and a pugnacious marmalade cat. Her erotic fiction has appeared in many collections including *Girl Crazy, Best Women's Erotica '09, '08* and *'07*, and more.

K. D. GRACE lives in England with her husband. She is passionate about nature, writing, and sex—not necessarily in that order. She entertains herself with Chinese martial arts, long, thought-provoking walks and extreme vegetable gardening. She has had erotica published in volumes from Black Lace, Xcite Books and more.

LILY HARLEM won first prize in the LoveHoney Vulgari Award for Erotic Fiction with an American-themed story entitled "Madam President," and lives in Wales with her husband, two teenage children and an ever growing menagerie of rescued pets.

LOUISA HARTE's (louisaharte.com) work has won third place in For the Girls Erotic Fiction Competition 2008 and was voted a Weekly Winner and semifinalist in the 5th Better Sex Erotic Fiction Contest Fall 2008. A New Zealander, she finds inspiration from many places, including her thoughts, dreams and fantasies.

AIMEE HERMAN has been previously published by Oysters & Chocolate, *Cliterature Journal, Pregnant Moon Review,* and *Evoke Journal.*

KAY JAYBEE (kayjaybee.me.uk) is the author of the erotic anthology *The Collector,* a regular contributor to Oysters and Chocolate and has a number of stories published in antholgies from Cleis Press (*Lips Like Sugar, Lust, Best Women's Erotica 2007, 2008, 2009* and *Best Lesbian Romance 2009),* Black Lace, Xcite Books, Mammoth Books and Penguin.

KRISTINA LLOYD (kristinalloyd.wordpress.com) is the author of three erotic novels including the controversial Black Lace bestseller, *Asking for Trouble.* Her stories have appeared in numerous anthologies and her novels have been translated into German, Dutch and Japanese. She is described as "a fresh literary talent" who "writes sex with a formidable force."

SOMMER MARSDEN's (SmutGirl.blogspot.com) work has appeared in dozens of anthologies and she is the author of multiple books including *Double Booked* and *The Mighty Quinn*. She lives in Maryland where she drinks red wine, writes, runs, reads and is a bit obsessed when it comes to sex, emails and reality TV.

For **ANASTASIA MAVROMATIS,** writing is like oxygen, and sexuality is like chocolate frosting. Her erotic stories have appeared on websites including Oysters and Chocolate, and in print: *Scarlet Magazine* (UK) and *Girls on Top: Explicit Erotica for Women* (Cleis Press). She resides in Sydney, Australia, where she publishes *Lucrezia Magazine.*

After many failed attempts at writing for academia, wondering why supervisors kept cutting out the good bits of her thesis, **LOZ MCKEEN** has only recently found her niche writing erotic fiction. She lives in Tasmania, Australia, with her husband and son.

AIMEE PEARL is a kinky bisexual exhibitionist who lives in San Francisco. She enjoys bossy perverts, gender rebels and assorted sexual misfits; her writing is much more fact than fiction. Aimee's erotic stories have appeared in *Best Lesbian Erotica 2008, On Our Backs* magazine, and *Longing, Lust, and Love.*

Called a "literary siren" by Good Vibrations, **ALISON TYLER** (alisontyler.com) is naughty and she knows it. Her sultry short stories have appeared in more than one hundred anthologies. She is the author of more than twenty-five erotic novels, and the editor of more than fifty explicit anthologies.

ABOUT THE EDITOR

VIOLET BLUE (tinynibbles.com) is a blogger, high-profile tech personality, award-winning, best-selling author and editor of more than two dozen books in five languages, podcaster, web TV show GETV reporter, technology futurist, and sex-positive pundit in mainstream media (such as CNN and "The Tyra Banks Show"). Blue is the sex columnist for the *San Francisco Chronicle* with a weekly column titled "Open Source Sex" and has a podcast of the same name with more than eight million downloads and counting. Blue is also a Forbes Web Celeb and one of *Wired*'s Faces of Innovation. She writes for media outlets such as *Forbes, O: The Oprah Magazine* and UN sponsored international health organization, RH Reality Check. Violet lectures to cyberlaw classes at UC Berkeley, human sexuality programs at UCSF and tech conferences (ETech and SXSW), in addition to sex crisis counselors at community teaching institutions and Google Tech Talks. Blue's tech blog is techyum.com and she publishes DRM-free audio and e-books at DigitaPub.com.